PHILIP JOSÉ FARMER
STATIONS OF THE
NIGHTMARE

TOR

A Tom Doherty Associates Book
Distributed by Pinnacle Books, New York

Copyright© 1982 by Philip José Farmer

A Tor Book

First printing: February, 1982

ISBN: 48-522-0

Cover Art by Greg Theakston

Interior Illustrations by: Peter Kuper

Printed in the United States of America

Distributed by
Pinnacle Books, Inc.
1430 Broadway
New York, N.Y. 10018

Acknowledgements:

STATIONS OF THE NIGHTMARE has been published
serially as follows: *The Two-Edged Gift*, in *Continuum I*,
copyright © 1974, by Roger Elwood; *The Startouched*, in
Continuum II, copyright © 1975, by Roger Elwood; *The
Evolution of Paul Eyre*, in *Continuum II*, copyright ©
1975, by Roger Elwood; *Passing On*, in *Continuum IV*,
copyright © 1975, by Roger Elwood. *Osiris on Crutches*
was published originally in *New Dimensions VI*
copyright © 1976, by Robert Silverberg.

*This is for Bill Rotsler, the bushy-bearded Bull of
Bashan and Calid Caliph of California.*

Philip José Farmer

STATIONS OF THE
NIGHTMARE

Part 1: THE TWO-
EDGED GIFT

CHAPTER ONE

PAUL EYRE shot a flying saucer.

On this bright morning, he was walking through a farmer's field. Ahead of him was the edge of a woods bisected by a small creek. Riley, the setter, had just stiffened. Nose down, crouched low, seeming to vibrate, he pointed toward the magnet, the invisible quail. Paul Eyre's heart pumped a little faster. Ahead of Riley, a few yards away, was a bush. Behind it should be the covey.

They broke loose with that racket that had made him jump so when he was a novice. It was as if the earth had given violent birth to several tiny planets. But there was not the dozen or so he had expected. Only two. The lead one was much larger than the other, so much larger that he did jump then. He knew as the shotgun roared and kicked that it was not a bird.

The concentrated pattern of his modified choke must have hit the thing squarely. It fell away at a forty-five degree angle instead of dropping as a dead bird drops, and it crashed through the lower branches of a tree on the outskirts of the woods.

Automatically, he had fired the second barrel at the trailing bird. And he had missed it.

The thing had rocketed up like a quail. But it had been dark and about two feet long. Or two feet wide. His finger had squeezed on the trigger even as his mind had squeezed on the revelation that it was not a winged creature.

It wasn't a creature, he thought, but a made thing. More like a huge clay pigeon than anything else.

He looked around. Riley was a white and black streak, running as if a cougar were after him. He made no noise. He seemed to be conserving his breath as if he knew he'd need every atom of oxygen he could get. Behind him was a trail of excrement. Ahead of him, over half a mile up the slope, was a white farmhouse and two dark-red barns.

Roger, Paul's son, had spoken of mines which flew up into the air before exploding. This thing had not been attached to a chain nor had it blown up. It could be a dud. But there had been no blast as it soared up. Perhaps the noise of his shotgun had covered it.

He shook his head. It could not have been anything like that. Unless . . . Had some vicious person put it in the field just to kill hunters? Senseless violence was on the increase in this God-forsaking country.

The situation was much like that of a car that refused to run. You could think about it all you wanted to and make mental images of what was wrong. But until you opened the hood and looked at the engine, you would not be able to make a definite analysis. So he would open the hood.

He walked forward. The only sound was the northwest wind, gentle here because the woods broke it. The bluejay and the crows that had been so noisy before he had fired were quiet. There was the bluejay, sitting on a tree branch. It seemed frozen with shock.

He was cautious but not afraid, he told himself. He had been afraid only three times in his life. When his father had deserted him, when his mother had died, and when Mavice had said she was leaving him. And these three events had taught him that nothing was as bad as he'd thought it at the time and that it was stupid, illogical to fear. He and his brothers and sisters and mother had gotten along without his father.

His mother's death had actually made his life easier. And Mavice had not left him.

"Only the unimaginative, of whom you are the king, have no fear," Tincrowdor had told him. But what did that effete egg-head know of real life or real men?

Nevertheless, he hesitated. He could just walk away, round up the dog, and hunt elsewhere. Or, better, tell Smith that someone had planted a strange mechanical device in his field.

Perhaps, though he did not like to admit it, his sight had betrayed him. Behind his glasses were fifty-four-year-old eyes. He was in good shape, better than most men twenty years younger. Much better than that Tincrowdor, who sat on his tocus all day while he typed away on his crazy stories.

Still, he had been informed by the optometrist that he needed a new prescription. He had not told anyone about this. He hated to admit to anyone that he had a weakness, and that anyone included himself. When he had a chance to get fitted with new lenses, with no one except the doctor the wiser, he'd go. Perhaps he should not have put it off so long.

He resumed walking slowly across the field. Once, he looked toward the farmhouse. Riley, his pace undiminished, was still headed toward it. When he caught Riley, he'd rap him a few on the nose and shame him. If he were ruined by this, he'd get rid of him. He couldn't see feeding something that was useless. The hound ate more than he was worth as it was.

He could imagine what Mavice would say about that. "You're going to retire in eleven years. Would you want us to give you away or send you to the gas chamber because you're useless?"

And he'd say, "But I won't be. I'll be working as hard as ever on my own business after I've retired."

He was ten feet from the wood when the yellow haze drifted out from it.

CHAPTER TWO

He stopped. It couldn't be pollen at this time of the year. And no pollen ever glowed.

Moreover, it was coming with too much force to be driven by the wind. For the second time, he hesitated. The thick yellow luminance looked so much like gas. He thought about the sheep that had been killed in Nevada or Utah when the army nerve gas had escaped. Could—But no . . . that was ridiculous.

The shimmering haze spread out, and he was in it. For a few seconds, he held his breath. Then he released it and laughed. The stuff blew away from his face and closed in again. Here and there, some bits sparkled. Before he reached the trees, he saw tiny blobs form on the grass, on his hands, and on the gun barrels. They looked like gold-colored mercury. When he ran his hand over the barrels, the stuff accumulated at the ends into two large drops. They ran like mercury into the cup formed by his palm.

Its odor made him wrinkle his nose and snap it to the ground. It smelled like spermatic fluid.

It was then that he noticed that he had not reloaded. He was mildly shocked. He had never missed reloading immediately after firing. In fact, he did it so automatically that he never even thought about it. He was more upset than he had realized.

Abruptly, the haze or fog, or whatever it was, disappeared. He looked around. The grass for about twenty feet behind him was faintly yellow.

He went on. A branch, broken off by the thing, lay before him. Ahead was the dense and silent wood. He pushed through the tangles of thorn bushes, from which he had flushed out so many rabbits. And there was one now, a big buck behind the thorns. It saw him, saw that it was seen, but it did not move. He crouched down to look at it. Its black eyes looked glazed, and its brown fur scintillated here and there with yellowness. It was in the shade, so the sun could not be responsible for the glints.

He poked at it, but it did not move. And

now he could see that it was trembling violently.

A few minutes later, he was at the place where the thing would have landed if it had continued its angle of descent. The bushes were undisturbed; the grass, unbent.

An hour passed. He had thoroughly covered the woods on his side of the creek and found nothing. He waded through the waters, which were nowhere deeper than two feet, and started his search through the woods on that side. He saw no yellow mercury, which meant one of two things. Either the thing had not come here or else it had quit expelling the stuff. That is, if the stuff *had* been expelled from it. It might just be a coincidence that the stuff had appeared at the same time the thing had disappeared. A coincidence, however, did not seem likely.

Then he saw a single drop of the mercury, and he knew that it was still . . . bleeding? He shook his head. Why would he think of that word? Only living creatures could be *wounded*. He had *damaged* it.

He whirled. Something had splashed behind him. Through a small break in the vegetation, he could see something round, flat, and black shooting from the middle of the creek. He had seen it before at a distance and had thought it was the top of a slightly rounded boulder just covered by the creek. His eyes *were* going bad.

He recrossed the creek and followed a

trail of water which dwindled away suddenly. He looked up, and something—it—dropped down behind a bush. There was a crashing noise, then silence.

So it was alive. No machine moved like that, unless . . .

What would Tincrowdor say if he told him that he had seen a flying saucer?

Common sense told him to say nothing to anybody about this. He'd be laughed at, and people would think he was going insane. Or suffering from premature senility, like his father.

The thought seemed to drive him crazy for a minute. Shouting, he plunged through the bushes and the thorn tangles. When he was under the tree from which the thing had dropped, he stopped. His heart was hammering, and he was sweating. There was no impression in the soft moisture-laden ground; nothing indicated that a large heavy object had fallen onto it.

Something moved to the right at the corner of his eye. He turned and shot once, then again. Pieces of bushes flew up, and bits of bark showered. He reloaded—he wasn't about to forget this time—and moved slowly toward the base of the bush at which the thing seemed to have been. But it wasn't there anymore, if it had ever been there.

A few feet further, he suddenly got dizzy. He leaned against a tree. His blood was thrumming in his ear, and the trees and bushes were melting. Perhaps the yellow stuff *was* some kind of nerve gas.

He decided to get out of the woods. It wasn't fear but logic that had made him change his mind. And no one had seen him retreat.

Near the edge of the woods, he stopped. He no longer felt dizzy, and the world had regained its hardness. It was true that only he would know he had quit, but he wouldn't ever again be able to think of himself as a real man. No, by God—and he told himself he wasn't swearing when he said that—he would see this out.

He turned and saw through the screen of bushes something white move out from behind a tree. It looked like the back of a woman's torso. She wore nothing; he could see the soft white skin and the indentation of the spine. The hips were not visible. Then the back of the head, black hair down to the white shoulders, appeared.

He shouted at the woman, but she paid no attention. When he got to the tree where she had first appeared, he could no longer see her. Some of the grass was still rising, and some leaves had been distorted.

An hour later, Paul Eyre gave up. Had he just thought he'd seen a woman? What would a woman be doing naked in these woods? She couldn't have been with a lover, because she and the man would have gotten out of the woods the first time he'd fired his shotgun.

On the way back, he thought he saw something big and tawny at a distance. He crouched down and opened the bush in front of him. About thirty yards off, going behind an almost solid tangle, was the back of an animal. It was yellowish brown and had a long tufted tail. And if he hadn't known it was impossible, he would have said that it was the rear end of an African lion. No, a lioness.

A moment later, he saw the head of a woman.

She was where the lion would be it if stood up on its hind legs and presented its head.

The woman was in profile, and she was the most beautiful he had ever seen.

He must be suffering from some insidious form of Asiatic flu. That would explain everything. In fact, it was the only explanation.

He was sure of it when he got to the edge of the trees. The field was covered with red flowers and at the other side, which seemed to be miles away, was a glittering green city.

The vision lasted only three or four seconds. The flowers and the city disappeared, and the field, as if it were a rubber band, snapped back to its real dimensions.

He could hear it snap.

Ten minutes later, he was at the farm-house.

Riley greeted him by biting him.

CHAPTER THREE

Eyre parked the car in front of his house. The driveway was blocked with a car to which was hitched a boat trailer, a motorcycle lacking a motor, and a Land Rover on top of which was a half-built camper. Behind it was a large garage crammed with machines, tools, supplies, old tires, and outboard motors in the process of being repaired.

Thirteen-thirty-one Wizman Court was in an area which once had been all residential. Now the huge old mansion across the street was a nursing home; the houses next to it had been torn down and buildings for a veterinarian and his kennels were almost completed. Eyre's own house had looked

large enough and smart enough when he
and Mavice had moved into it twenty years
ago. It looked tiny, mean, and decaying now
and had looked so for ten years.

Paul Eyre, until this moment, had never
noticed that. Though he felt crowded at
times, he attributed this to too many
people, not the smallness of the house. Once
he got rid of his son and daughter, the
house would again become comfortable.
And the house was paid for. Besides taxes,
maintenance, and the utilities, it cost him
nothing. If the neighborhood was run down
somewhat, so much the better. His neighbors did not complain because he was con-
ducting his own repair business here.

Until now, he had not thought anything
about its appearance. It was just a house.
But now he noticed that the grass on the
tiny lawn was uncut, the wooden shutters
needed painting, the driveway was a mess,
and the sidewalk was cracked.

He got out of the car and picked up his
shotgun and bag with his left hand. The
right hand was heavily bandaged. The old
ladies sitting on the side porch waved and
called out to him, and he waved back at
them. They sat like a bunch of ancient
crows on a branch. Time was shooting them
down, one by one. There was an empty
chair at the end of the row, but it would be
occupied by a newcomer soon enough. Mr.
Ridgley had sat there until last week when

he had been observed one afternoon urinating over the railing into the rosebushes below. He was, according to the old ladies, now locked up in his room on the third floor. Eyre looked up and saw a white face with tobacco-stained moustaches pressed against the bars over the window.

He waved. Mr. Ridgley stared. The mouth below the moustaches drooled. Angry, Paul Eyre turned away. His mother had stared out of that window for several weeks, and then she had disappeared. But she had lived to be eighty-six before she had become senile. That was forgivable. What he could not forgive, nor forget, was that his father had only been sixty when his brain had hardened and his reason had slid off it.

He went up the wooden unpainted steps off the side of the front porch. It was no longer just a porch. He had enclosed it and Roger now used it for a bedroom. Roger, as usual, had neglected to make up the bed-couch. Four years in the Marines, including a hitch in Viet Nam, had not made him tidy.

Eyre growled at Roger as he entered the front room. Roger, a tall thin blond youth, was sitting on the sofa and reading a college textbook. He said, "Oh, Mom said she'd do it." He stared at his father's hand. "What happened?"

"Riley went mad, and I had to shoot him."

Mavice, coming in from the kitchen, said, "Oh, my God! You *shot* him!"

Tears ran down Roger's cheeks.

"Why would you do that?"

Paul waved his right hand. "Didn't you hear me? He bit me! He was trying for my throat!"

"Why would he do that?" Mavice asked.

"You sound like you don't believe me!" Paul said. "For God's sake, isn't anyone going to ask me how badly he bit me? Or worry that I might get rabies?"

Roger wiped away the tears and looked at the bandages. "You've been to a doctor," he said. "What'd he say about it?"

"Riley's head has been shipped to the state lab," Paul said. "Do you have any idea what it's going to be like if I have to have rabies shots? Anyway, it's fatal! Nobody ever survived rabies!"

Mavice's hand shot to her mouth and from behind it came strangled sounds. Her light blue eyes were enormous.

"Yeah, and horseshoes hung over the door bring good luck," Roger said. "Why don't you come out of the nineteenth century, Dad? Look at something besides outboard motors and the TV. The rate of recovery from rabies is very high."

"So I only had one year of college," Paul said. "Is that any reason for my smartass son to sneer at me? Where would you be if it wasn't for the G.I. Bill?"

"You go to college to get a degree, not an education," Roger said. "You have to educate yourself, all your life."

"For Heaven's sake, you two," Mavice said. "Quit this eternal bickering. And sit down, Paul. Take it easy. You look terrible!"

He jerked his arm away and said, "I'm all right." But he sat down. The mirror behind the sofa had showed him a short, thin but broad-shouldered man with smooth pale brown hair, a high forehead, bushy sandy eyebrows, blue eyes behind octagonal rimless spectacles, a long nose, a thick brown moustache, and a round cleft chin.

His face did look like a mask. Tincrowdor had said that anyone who wore glasses should never sport a moustache. Together, these gave a false-face appearance. That remark had angered him then. Now it reminded him that he was looking forward to seeing Tincrowdor. Maybe he had some answers.

"What about a beer, Dad?" Roger said. He looked contrite.

"That'd help, thanks," Paul said. Roger hurried off to the kitchen while Mavice stood looking down at him. Even when both were standing up, she was still looking down on him. She was at least four inches taller.

"You don't really think Riley had rabies?" she said. "He seemed all right this morning."

"Not really. He wasn't foaming at the

mouth or anything like that. Something scared him in the woods, scared him witless, and he attacked me. He didn't know what he was doing."

Mavice sat down in a chair across the room. Roger brought in the beer. Paul drank it gratefully, though its amber color reminded him of the yellow stuff. He looked at Mavice over the glass. He had always thought she was very good-looking, even if her face was somewhat long. But, remembering the profile of the woman in the woods, he saw that she was very plain indeed, if not ugly. Any woman's face would look bad now that he had seen that glory among the trees.

The front door slammed, and Glenda walked in from the porch. He felt vaguely angry. He always did when he saw her. She had a beautiful face, a feminization of his, and a body which might have matched the face but never would. It was thin and nearly breastless, though she was seventeen. The spine was shaped like a question mark; one shoulder was lower than the other; the legs looked as thin as piston rods.

She stopped and said, "What happened?" Her voice was deep and husky, sexy to those who heard it without seeing her.

Mavice and Roger told her what had taken place. Paul braced himself for a storm of tears and accusations, since she loved Riley dearly. But she said nothing about him. She seemed concerned only about her father. This not only surprised him. It angered him.

Why was he angry? he thought.

And· he understood, then, that it was because she was a living reproach. If it weren't for him, she would not be twisted; she'd be a tall straight and beautiful girl. His anger had been his way of keeping this knowledge from himself.

He was amazed that he had not known this before. How could he have been so blind?

He began sweating. He shifted on the sofa as if he could move his body away from the revelation. He felt the beginning of a panic. What had opened his eyes so suddenly? Why had he only now, today, noticed how ugly and mean the house was, how frightened and repulsed he was by the old people across the street, and why Glenda had angered him when he should have shown her nothing but tenderness?

He knew why. Something had happened to him in the woods, and it was probably the stuff which had fallen on him, the stuff expelled by the thing. But how could it have given him this insight? It scared him. It made him feel as if he were losing something very dear.

He almost yielded to the desire to tell them everything. No, they would not believe him. Oh, they'd believe that he had seen those things. But they would think that he was going crazy, and they would be frightened. If he would shoot Riley while in a fit, he might shoot them.

He became even more frightened. Many times, he had imagined doing just this. What if he lost control and the image shifted gears into reality?

He stood up. "I think I'll wash up and then go to bed for a while. I don't feel so good."

This seemed to astonish everybody.

"What's so strange about that?" he said loudly.

"Why, Dad, you've always had to be forced to bed when you've been sick," Glenda said. "You just won't admit that you can get ill, like other people. You act as if you were made of stone, as if microbes bounced off of you."

"That's because I'm not a hyper—a hyper—a what-you-call-it, a goldbricker, like some people," he said.

"A hypochondriac," Glenda and Roger said at the same time.

"Don't look at me when you say that," Mavice said, glaring at him. "You know I have a chronic bladder infection. I'm not faking it. Dr. Wells told you that himself when you called him to find out if I was lying. I was never so embarrassed in all my life."

The shrill voice was coming from a long

way off. Glenda was becoming even more crooked, and Roger was getting thinner and taller.

The doorway to the bedroom moved to one side as he tried to get through it. He couldn't make it on two legs, so he got down on all fours. If he was a dog, he'd have a more solid footing, and maybe the doorway would be so confused by the sudden change of identities it would hold still long enough for him to get through it.

He heard Mavice's scream and barked an assurance that he was all right. Then he was protesting to Mavice and Roger that he didn't want to stand up, but they had hoisted him up and were guiding him toward the bed. It didn't matter then, since he had gotten through. Let the doorway move around all it wanted now; he had fooled it. You could teach an old dog new tricks.

Later, he heard Mavice's voice drilling through the closed door. Here he was, trying to sleep off whatever was ailing him, and she was screaming like a parrot. Nothing would ever get her to lower that voice. Too many decibels from a unibelle, he thought. Which was a strange thought, even if he was an engineer. But he wished she would tone down or, even better, shut up. Forever. He knew that it wasn't her fault, since both her parents had been somewhat deaf during her childhood. But they were dead now, and she had no logical reason to keep on screaming as if she were trying to wake the dead.

Why hadn't he ever said anything about it? Because he nourished the resentment, fed it with other resentments. And then, when the anger became too great, he in turn screamed at her. But it was always about other things. He had never told her how grating her voice was.

He sat up suddenly and then got out of bed. He was stronger now, and the doorway was no longer alive. He walked out into the little hall and said, "What are you saying to Morna?"

Mavice looked at him in surprise and put her hand over the receiver. "I'm calling off tonight. You're too sick to have company."

"No, I'm not," he said. "I'm all right. You tell her to come on over as planned."

Mavice's penciled eyebrows rose. "All right, but if I'd insisted they come, you would have gotten mad at me."

"I got work to do," he said, and headed toward the rear exit.

"With that bandage on your hand?" Mavice said.

He threw both hands up into the air and went into the living room. Roger was sitting in a chair and holding a textbook while watching TV.

"How can you study freshman calculus while Matt Dillon is shooting up the place?"

Paul Eyre said.

"Every time a gun goes off and a redskin bites the dust, another equation becomes clear," Roger said.

"What the hell does that mean?"

"I don't know what it means," Roger said calmly. "I just know it works."

"I don't understand you," Paul said. "When I was studying I had to have absolute quiet."

"Didn't you listen to the radio while you were hitting the books?"

Paul seemed surprised.

"No."

"Well, I was raised this way," Roger said. "All my friends were. Maybe we learned how to handle two or more things simultaneously. Maybe that's where the generation gap is. We take in many different things at once and see the connections among them. But you only saw one thing at a time."

"So that makes you better than us?"

"Different, anyway," Roger said. "Dad, you ought to read MacLuhan. But then . . ."

"But then what?"

"But you never read anything but the local newspaper, sports magazines, and stuff connected with your work."

"I don't have time," Paul said. "I'm holding down a job at Trackless and working eight hours a day on my own business. You know that."

"Leo Tincrowdor used to do that, and he read three books a week. But then he wants to know."

"Yeah, he knows so much, but if his car breaks down, can he fix it himself? No, he has to call in an expensive mechanic. Or get me to do it for him for nothing."

"Nobody's perfect," Roger said. "Anyway, he's more interested in finding out how the universe works and why our society is breaking down and what can be done to repair it."

"It wouldn't be breaking down if people like him weren't trying to break it down!"

"You would have said the same thing a hundred years ago," Roger said. "You think things are in a mess now; you should read about the world in 1874. The good old days. My history professor—"

Paul strode from the room and into the kitchen. He never drank more than two beers a day, but today was different. And *how* it was different. The top of the can popped open, reminding him of the sound when the field had snapped back to normalcy. Now *there* was a connection which Roger, nobody else in the world, in fact, would have made. He wished he had stayed home to catch up on his work instead of indulging himself in a quail hunt.

CHAPTER FOUR

At seven, the Tincrowdors walked in. Usually, Paul kept them waiting, since he always had to finish up on a motor in the garage. By the time he had washed up, Leo had had several drinks and Morna and Mavice were engaged in one of their fast-moving female conversations. Leo was happy enough talking to Roger or Glenda or, if neither were there, happy to be silent. He did not seem to resent Paul's always showing up late. Paul suspected that he would have been content if he never showed up. Yet, he always greeted him with a smile. If he had been drinking much, he also had some comment which sounded funny but which concealed a joke at Paul's expense.

Tonight, however, Paul was in the living room when they arrived. He jumped up and kissed Morna enthusiastically. He always kissed good-looking women if they would let him; it gave him a sense of innocent infidelity, outside of the sheer pleasure of kissing. Morna had to bend down a little, like Mavice, but she put more warmth into it than Mavice. Yet she was always, well, often, chewing him out in defense of her friend, Mavice.

Leo Queequeg Tincrowdor enclosed Paul's hand with his over-sized one and squeezed. He was a six footer with heavy bones and a body that had once been muscular but now was turning to fat. His once auburn hair was white and thinning. Below protruding bars of bone, his strange leaf-green eyes, the balls bloodshot, looked at and through Paul. His cheeks were high and red. His beard was a mixture of gray, black, and red. He had a deep voice the effect of which was lessened by a tendency to slur when drinking. And Paul had only seen him twice when he hadn't been drinking. He pushed ahead of him a balloon of bourbon. When he had money, it was Waller's Special Reserve. When he was broke, it was cheap whiskey cut with lemon juice. Evidently, he had recently received a story check. The balloon had an expensive odor.

"Sit down, Leo." Ritualistically, Eyre

asked, "What'll it be? Beer or whiskey?"

Ritualistically, Tincrowdor answered, "Bourbon. I only drink beer when I can't get anything better."

When Paul returned with six ounces of Old Kentucky Delight on ice, he found Tincrowdor handing out two of his latest softcovers to Roger and Glenda. He felt a thrust of jealousy as they exclaimed over the gifts. How could the kids enjoy that trash?

"What's this?" he said, handing Leo his drink and then taking the book from Glenda. The cover showed a white man in a cage surrounded by some green-skinned women, all naked, reaching through the bars for the man. In the background was a mountain vaguely resembling a lion with a woman's head. On top of the head was a white Grecian temple with small figures, holding knives around another figure stretched out on an altar.

"*Sphinxes Without Secrets,*" Leo said. "It's about a spaceman who lands on a planet inhabited by women. The males died off centuries before, mostly from heartbreak. A chemist, a women's lib type, had put a substance in the central food plant which made the men unable to have erections."

"What?" Mavice said. She laughed, but her face went red.

"It's an old idea," Leo said. He sipped the

bourbon and shuddered. "But I extrapolate to a degree nobody else has ever done before. Or is capable of doing. It's very realistic. Too much so for the *Busiris Journal-Star*. Their reviewer not only refused to write a review, he sent me a nasty letter. Nothing libelous. Old Potts doesn't have the guts for that."

"If there weren't any men, how could they have babies?" Paul said.

"Chemically induced parthenogenesis. Virgin birth caused by chemicals. It's been done with rabbits and theoretically could be done with humans. I don't doubt that the Swedes have done it, but they're keeping quiet about it. They have no desire to be martyrs."

"That's blasphemy!" Paul said. His face felt hot, and he had a momentary image of himself throwing Tincrowdor out on his rear. "There's only been one virgin birth, and that was divinely inspired."

"Inspired? That sounds like a blow job," Tincrowdor said. "No, I apologize for that remark. When among the aborigines, respect their religion. However, I will point out that if Jesus was the result of parthenogenesis, he should have been a woman. All parthenogenetically stimulated offspring are females. Females only carry the X chromosome, you know. Or do you? It's the male's Y chromosome that determines that the baby be a male."

"But God is, by the definition of God, all-powerful," Glenda said. "So why couldn't He have, uh, inserted a sort of spiritual Y chromosome?"

Tincrowdor laughed and said, "Very good, Glenda. You'd make an excellent science-fiction author, God help you."

"Anyway, every culture has its deviates, and this lesbian society was no exception. So a few perverts were not repulsed by the spaceman. Instead, he was to them a most desirable sex object."

"How could a woman who wanted a man instead of a woman be a deviate?" Paul said.

"Deviation is determined by what the culture considers normal. When we were kids, going down was considered by almost everybody to be a perversion, and you could get put in jail for twenty years or more if caught doing it. But in our lifetime, we've seen this attitude change. By 2010, anything between consenting adults will be acceptable. But there are still millions in this country who think the only God-favored way is for the woman to lie on her back with the man on top. And would you believe it, there are millions who won't undress in front of each other or keep a light on during intercourse. These sexual dinosaurs, for that's what they are, will be extinct in another fifty years. Could I have another drink?"

Paul Eyre glared at his wife. She must have been confiding in Morna. Tincrowdor had made it obvious that he was talking about the Eyres. Was nothing sacred anymore?

Nor did he like this kind of talk before Glenda.

He said, "Roger, will you get him another whiskey?"

Roger left reluctantly. Mavice said, "So what happened to the spaceman?"

"He was a homosexual and wanted nothing to do with the woman who let him out of his cage. Scorned, she turned him in to the priestesses, and they sacrificed him. However, he was stuffed and put in a museum alongside a gorilla-type ape. Due to complaints from the Decency League, he was eventually fitted with a skirt to hide his nauseating genitals."

"What does the title mean?" Mavice said.

"That's from Oscar Wilde, who said that women were sphinxes without secrets."

"I like *that*!" Mavice said.

"Oscar Wilde was a queer," Morna said. "What would he know about women?"

"Being half-female, he knew more about them than most men," Tincrowdor said.

Paul wanted to get away from that subject. He leaned over and took the other book from Glenda. "*Osiris On Crutches*. What does that mean? Or maybe I'm better off if I don't ask."

"Osiris was an ancient Egyptian god. His evil brother, Set, tore him apart and scattered the pieces all over earth. But Osiris' wife, Isis, and his son, Horus, collected the pieces and put them back together again and revivified him. My book tells the story in detail. For a long time, Osiris was missing a leg, so he hopped around earth on crutches looking for it. That wasn't the only thing he was missing. His nose couldn't be found, either, so Isis stuck his penis over his nasal cavity. This explains why Osiris is sometimes depicted as being ibis-headed. The ibis was a bird with a long beak. An early Pharoah thought this was obscene and so ordered all artists to change the penis into a beak.

"Anyway, after many adventures, Osiris found his leg but wished he hadn't. He got a lot more sympathy as a cripple. He found his nose, too, but the tribe that had it refused to give it up. Since it was a piece of a divine being, they'd made a god of it. It was giving them good crops, both of wheat and babies, and it was dispensing excellent, if somewhat nasal, oracles.

"Osiris blasted them with floods and lightning bolts, and so scared them into returning his nose. But he would have been better off if he hadn't interfered with their religious customs. His nose elongated and swelled when he was sexually excited, which was most of the time, since he was a god. And he breathed through his penis."

"For heaven's sake!" Paul said. "That's pornography! No wonder Potts won't review your books!"

"They said the same thing about Aristophanes, Rabelais, and Joyce," Tincrowdor said.

"I'm just as glad that the paper won't review his books," Morna said. "It would be so embarrassing. I'm on good terms with our neighbors, but if they found out what he wrote, we'd be ostracized. Fortunately, they don't read science-fiction."

Leo was silent for a moment, and then he looked at Paul's bandaged hand. "Morna said your dog bit you today. You had to shoot him."

He made it sound like an accusation.

"It was terrible," Mavice said. "Roger cried."

"Tears over a dog from a man who's booby-trapped cans of food to blow up infants," Tincrowdor said.

Roger handed him his drink and said, "Those same little kids were the ones tossing grenades in our trucks!"

"Yeah, I know," Tincrowdor said. "Don't criticize a man unless you've walked a mile in his G.I. boots. I shot some twelve-year-olds in World War II. But they were shooting at me. I suppose the principle's the same. It's the practice I don't like. Did you ever see your victims, Roger? After the explosions, I mean."

"No, I'm not morbid," Roger said.

"I saw mine. I'll never forget them."

"You better lay off the booze," Morna said. "You've been insulting and now you're going to get sloppy sentimental."

"Advice from the world's champion insulter," Tincrowdor said. "She calls it being frank. Does it hurt, Paul? The bite, I mean."

"You're the first person who's asked me that," Paul said. "My family's more concerned about the dog than me."

"That's not true!" Mavice said. "I'm terribly worried about rabies!"

"If he starts foaming at the mouth, shoot him," Tincrowdor said.

"That's not funny!" Morna said. "I saw a kid that'd been bit by a dog when I was working in the hospital. He didn't get rabies, but the vaccination made him suffer terribly. Don't you worry, Paul. There's not much chance Riley had hydrophobia. He hadn't had any contact with other animals. Maybe the postmortem will show he had a tumor on his brain. Or something."

"Maybe he just didn't like Paul," Tincrowdor said.

Paul understood that Tincrowdor was speaking not only for the dog but for himself.

"I once wrote a short story called *The Vaccinators from Vega*. The Vegans appeared one day in a great fleet with weapons against which Earth was powerless. The Vegans were bipedal but hairy and had bad breaths because they ate only meat. They were, in fact, descended from dogs, not apes. They had big black eyes soft with love, and they were delighted because we had so many telephone poles. And they had come to save the universe, not to conquer our planet. They said a terrible disease would soon spread throughout the galaxy, but they would be able to immunize everybody. The Earthlings objected against forcible vaccination, but the Vegans pointed out that the Earthlings themselves had provided the precedent.

"After they had given everybody a shot, they departed, taking with them some of the terrestrial artifacts they thought valuable. These weren't our great works of art or sports cars or atom bombs. They took fire hydrants and flea powder. Ten weeks later all members of homo sapiens dropped dead. The Vegans hadn't told us that *we* were the dreaded disease. Mankind was too close to interstellar travel."

"Don't you ever write anything good about people?" Paul said.

"The people get the kind of science-fiction writer they deserve."

At least, that's what Paul thought he said. Tincrowdor was getting more unintelligble with every sip.

"Sure, I've written a number of stories about good people. They always get killed. Look at what happened to Jesus. Anyway, one of my stories is a glorification of mankind. It's entitled *The Hole in the Coolth*. God is walking around in the Garden in the coolth of the evening. He's just driven Adam and Eve out of Eden, and He's wondering if He shouldn't have killed them instead. You see, there are no animals in the world outside. They're all in the Garden, very contented. The Garden is a small place, but there's no worry about the beasts getting too numerous. God's ecosystem is perfect; the births just balance the deaths.

"But now there's nothing except accident, disease, and murder to check the growth of human population. No saber-tooth cats or poisonous snakes. No sheep, pigs, or cattle, either. That means that mankind will be vegetarians, and if they want protein they'll have to eat nuts. In a short time they'll have spread out over the earth, and since they won't discover agriculture for another two thousand years, they'll eat all the nuts. Then they'll look over the fence around the Garden and see all those four-footed edibles there. There goes the neighborhood. The Garden will be ruined; the flowers all tromped flat; the animals exterminated in an orgy of carnivorousness. Maybe He should change

His mind and burn them with a couple of lightning strokes. He needs the practice anyway."

"Another thing that bothers God is that He can't stop thinking about Eve. God receives the emotions of all his creatures, as if he's a sort of spiritual radio set. When an elephant is constipated, He feels its agony. When a baboon has been rejected by its pack, He feels its loneliness and sadness. When a wolf kills a fawn, He feels the horror of the little deer and the gladness of the wolf. He also tastes the deliciousness of the meat as it goes down the wolf's mouth. And He appreciates the animals' feelings for sex.

"But human beings have a higher form of sex. It involves psychology, too, and this is so much better. On the other hand, due to psychology, it's often much inferior. But Adam and Eve haven't existed long enough to get their psyches too messed up. So God, as a sort of mental peeping tom, enjoys Adam's and Eve's coupling. Qualitatively, Adam and Eve are so far ahead of the other creations, there's no comparison.

"When Adam takes Eve in his arms, God does too. But in this eternal triangle, no cuckolding is involved. Besides, God had made Eve first.

"But when Adam and Eve were run out of Eden, God decided to dampen the power of His reception from them. He'll stay tuned in, but He'll be getting only faint signals. That means He won't be getting full ecstasy of their mating. On the other hand, He won't be suffering so much because of their grief and loneliness. The two are deep in Africa and heading south, and the signals are getting weaker. About the only thing He can pick up is a feeling of sadness. Still, He sees Eve in His mind's eye, and He knows He's missing a lot. But He refuses to apply more of the divine juice. Better He should forget them for a while.

"He's walking along the fence, thinking these thoughts, when He feels a draft. The cold air of the world outside is blowing into the pleasant warm air of the Garden. This should not be, so God investigates. And he finds a hole dug under the golden, jewel-studded fence that rings Eden. He's astounded, because the hole has been dug from the Garden side. Somebody has gotten *out* of the Garden, and He doesn't understand this at all. He'd understand if somebody tried to get *in*. But *out!*

"A few minutes later, or maybe it was a thousand years later, since God, when deep in thought, isn't aware of the passage of time, he receives a change of feeling from Adam and Eve. They're joyous, and the grief at being kicked out of Eden is definitely less.

"God walks out of Eden and down into Africa to find out what's made the change.

He could be there in a nanosecond, but He prefers to walk. He finds Adam and Eve in a cave and two dogs and their pups standing guard at the entrance. The dogs snarl and bark at Him before they recognize Him. God pets them, looks inside the cave, and sees Adam and Eve with their children, Cain, Abel and a couple of baby girls. It was their sisters who would become Cain and Abel's wives, you know. But that's another story.

"God was touched. If human beings could gain the affections of dogs so much that they would leave the delights of Eden, literally dig their way out just to be with human, then humans must have something worthwhile. So He returned to the Garden and told the angel with the flaming sword to drive the other animals out.

"It'll be a mess," the angel said.

" 'Yes, I know,' God said. 'But if there aren't other animals around, those poor dogs will starve to death. They've got nothing but nuts to eat.' "

Paul and Mavice were shocked by such blasphemy. Roger and Glenda laughed. There was a tinge of embarrassment in their laughter, but it was caused by their parents' reaction.

Morna had laughed, but she said, "That's the man I have to live with! And when he's telling you about Osiris and God, he's telling you about himself!"

There was silence for a moment. Paul decided that now was his chance. "Listen, Leo, I had a dream this afternoon. It may be a great idea for you."

"O.K.," Tincrowdor said. He looked weary.

"You didn't sleep this afternoon," Mavice said. "You weren't in bed for more than a few minutes."

"I know if I slept or if I didn't. The dream must've been caused by what happened this morning. But it's wild. I dreamt I was hunting quail, just like I did this morning. I was on the same field, and Riley had just taken a point, like he did this morning. But from then on . . ."

Leo said nothing until Paul was finished. He asked Roger to fill his glass again. For a moment he twiddled his thumbs, and then he said, "The most amazing thing about your dream is that you dreamed it. It is too rich in imaginative details for you."

Paul opened his mouth to protest, but Tincrowdor held up his hand for silence.

"Morna has related to me dreams which you told Mavice about. You don't have many—rather, you don't remember many, and those few you do seem to you remarkable. But they're not. They're very poor stuff. You see, the more creative and imaginative a person, the richer and more original his dreams. Yes, I know that you do have a flair for engineering creativity.

You're always tinkering around on gadgets you've invented. In fact, you could have become fairly wealthy from some of them. But you either delayed too long applying for a patent, and so someone else beat you to it, or you never got around to building a model of your gadget or never finished it. Someone always got there ahead of you. Which is significant. You should look into why you dillydally and so fail. But then you don't believe in psychoanalysis, do you?''

"What's that got to do with this dream?" Paul said.

"Everything is connected, way down under, where the roots grope and the worms blind about and the gnomes tunnel through crap for gold. Even the silly chatter of Mavice and Morna about dress sizes and recipes and gossip about their friends is meaningful. You listen to them a while, if you can stand it, and you'll see they're not talking about what they seem to be talking about. Behind the mundane messages is a *secret* message, in a code which can be broken down if you work hard at it, and have the talent to understand it. Mostly they're S.O.S.'s, cryptic may-days."

"I like *that!*" Mavice said.

"Up your cryptic!" Morna said.

"What about the dream?" Paul said.

"As a lay analyst, I'm more of a layer—of eggs, unfortunately—than an analyzer. I don't know what your dream *means*. You'd have to go to a psychoanalyst for that, and of course you'd never do that because, one, it costs a lot of money, and two, you'd think people would think you were crazy.

"Well, you are, though suffering from that kind of insanity which is called *normalcy*. What I am interested in are the elements of your dream. The flying saucer, the gaseous golden blood from its wound, the sphinx, and the glittering green city."

"The sphinx?" Paul asked. "You mean the big statue by the pyramids? The lion with a woman's head?"

"Now, that's the Egyptian sphinx, and it's a he, not a she, by the way. I'm talking of the ancient Greek sphinx with a lion's body and lovely woman's breasts and face. Though the one you described seemed more like a leocentaur. It had a woman's trunk which joined the lion's body, lioness', to be exact, where the animal's neck should be."

"I didn't see anything like that!"

"You didn't see the entirety. But it's obvious that she was a leocentaur. Nor did you give her a chance to ask you the question. *What is it that in the morning goes on four legs, in the afternoon on two, and in the evening on three?* Oedipus answered the question and then killed her. You wanted to shoot her before she could open her mouth."

"What was the answer?" Mavice said.

"Man," Glenda said. "Typically anthropocentric and male chauvinistic."

"But these are not ancient times, and I'm sure she had a question relevant to this contemporary age. But you must have read about her sometime, maybe in school. Otherwise, why the image? And about the green city? Have you ever read the Oz books?"

"No, but I had to take Glenda and Roger to see the movie when they were young. Mavice was sick."

"He wouldn't let me see it on TV last month," Glenda said. "He said Judy Garland was an animal."

"She used *drugs*!" Paul said. "Besides, that picture is a lot of nonsense!"

"How like you to equate that poor suffering soul with vermin," Tincrowdor said. "And I suppose your favorite TV series, *Bonanza*, isn't fantasy? Or *The Music Man*, which you love so much? Or most of the stuff you read as the gospel truth in our right-wing rag, the *Busiris Journal-Star*?"

"You're not so smart," Paul said. "You haven't got the slightest idea what my dream means!"

"You're stung," Tincrowdor said. "No, if I was so smart, I'd be charging you twenty-five dollars an hour. However, I wonder if that *was* a dream. You didn't actually *see* all this out in that field? By the way, just where is it? I'd like to go out and investigate."

"You *are* crazy!" Paul said.

"I think we'd better go," Morna said. "Paul has such an awful yellow color."

Paul detested Tincrowdor at that moment and yet he did not want him to leave.

"Just a minute. Don't you think it'd make a great story?"

Tincrowdor sat back down. "Maybe. Let's say the saucer isn't a mechanical vehicle but a living thing. It's from some planet of some far-off star, of course. Martians aren't *de rigeur* anymore. Let's say the saucer-person lands here because it's going to seed this planet. The yellow stuff wasn't its blood but its spores or its eggs. When it's ready to spawn, or lay, it's in a vulnerable position, like a mother sea-turtle when it lays its eggs in the sand of a beach. It's not as mobile as it should be. A hunter comes across it at the critical moment, and he shoots it. The wound opens its womb or whatever, and it prematurely releases the eggs. Then, unable to take off in full flight, it hides. The hunter is a brave man or lacking imagination or both. So he goes into the woods after the saucerperson. It's still capable of projecting false images of itself; its electromagnetic field or whatever it is that enables it to fly through space, stimulates the brain of the alien biped that's hunting it. Images deep in the hunter's unconscious are evoked. The hunter thinks he sees a sphinx and a glittering green city.

"And the hunter has breathed in some of the spore-eggs. This is what the saucer-person desires, since the reproductive cycle is dependent on living hosts. Like sheep liver flukes. The eggs develop in larvae which feed on the host. Or perhaps they're not parasitic but symbiotic. They give the host something beneficial in return for his temporarily housing them. Maybe the incubating stage is a long and complicated one. The host can transmit the eggs or the larvae to other hosts.

"Have you been sneezing yellow, Paul?"

"In time, the larvae will mutate into something, maybe little saucers. Or another intermediate stage, something horrible and inimical. Maybe these take different forms, depending upon the chemistry of the hosts. In any event, in human beings the reaction is not just physical. It's psychosomatic. But the host is doomed, and he is highly infectious. Anybody who comes into contact with him is going to be filled with, become rotten with, the larvae. There's no chance of quarantining the hosts. Not in this age of great mobility. Mankind has invented the locomotive, the automobile, the airplane solely to make the trans-mission of the deadly larvae easier. At least, that's the viewpoint of the saucerperson.

"Doom, doom, doom!"

"Dumb, dumb, dumb," Morna said.

"Come on, Leo, let's go. You'll be snoring like a pig, and I won't be able to get a wink of sleep. He snores terribly when he's been drinking. I could kill him."

"Wait for time to do its work," Tincrowdor said. "I'm slowly killing myself with whiskey. It's the curse of the Celtic race. Booze, not the British, beat us. With which alliteration, I bid you bon voyage. Or von voyage. I'm part German, too."

"What are your Teutonic ancestors responsible for?" Morna said. "Your arrogance?"

CHAPTER FIVE

After the Tincrowdors had left, Mavice said, "You really should get to bed, Paul. You do look peaked. And we have to get up early tomorrow for church."

He didn't reply. His bowels felt as if an octopus had squeezed them in its death agony. He got to the bathroom just in time, but the pain almost yanked a scream from him. Then it was over. He became faint when he saw what was floating in the water. It was small, far too small to have caused such trouble. It was an ovoid about an inch long, and it was a dull yellow. For some reason, he thought of the story of the goose that laid golden eggs.

He began trembling. It was ten minutes

or more before he could flush it down, wash, and leave the bathroom. He had a vision of the egg dissolving in the pipes, being treated in the sewage plant, spreading its evil parts throughout the sludge, being transported to farms for fertilizer, being sucked up by the roots of corn, wheat, soy beans, being eaten, being carried around in the bodies of men and animals, being . . .

In the bedroom, Mavice tried to kiss him goodnight. He turned away. Was he infectious? Had that madman accidentally hit on the truth?

"Don't kiss me then," Mavice shrilled. "You never want to kiss me unless you want to go to bed with me. That's the only time I get any tenderness from you, if you can call it tenderness. But I'm just as glad. I have a bladder infection and you'd hurt me. After all, it's my wifely duty, no matter how sick I am. According to you, anyway."

"Shut up, Mavice," he said. "I'm sick. I don't want you to catch anything."

"Catch what? you said you felt all right. You don't have the flu, do you?"

"I don't know what I got," he said, and he groaned.

"Oh, Lord, I pray it's not the rabies," she said.

"It couldn't be. Morna said rabies doesn't act that fast."

"Then what is it?"

"I don't know," he said, and groaned again. "What is it Leo is so fond of quoting? *Whom the gods wish to destroy, they first make mad?*"

"What's that supposed to mean?" she said, but she softened. She kissed him on the cheek before he could object, and turned over away from him.

He lay awake a long time, and when he did sleep he had fitful dreams. They awoke him often, though he remembered few of them. But there was one of a glittering green city and a thing with a body which was part lioness and part woman and advancing toward him over a field of scarlet flowers.

CHAPTER SIX

Roger Eyre stood up and looked at Leo Tincrowdor. They were standing near the edge of a cornfield just off the Little Rome Road.

"They're the tracks of a big cat all right," he said. "A very big cat. If I didn't know better, I'd say they were a lion's or a tiger's. One that could fly."

"Your major is zoology, so you should know," Tincrowdor said. He looked up at the sky. "It's going to rain. I wish we had time to get casts. Do you think that if we went back to your house and got some plaster . . .?"

"It's going to be a heavy rain storm. No."

"Damn it, I should have at least brought a

camera. But I never dreamed of this. It's objective evidence. Your father isn't crazy, and that dream. . . . I thought he was telling more than a dream."

"You can't be serious," Roger said.

Tincrowdor pointed at the prints in the mud. "Your father was driving to work when he suddenly pulled the car over just opposite here. Three men in a car a quarter of a mile behind him saw him do it. They knew him, since they work at Trackless, too. They stopped and asked him if his car had broken down. He mumbled a few unintelligible words and then became completely catatonic. Do you think that and these tracks are just coincidence?"

Ten minutes later, they were in the Adler Sanitorium. As they walked down the hall, Tincrowdor said, "I went to Shomi University with Doctor Croker, so I should be able to get more out of him than the average doctor would tell. He thinks my books are a lot of crap, but we're both members of The Baker Street Irregulars and he likes me, and we play poker twice a month. Let me do the talking. Don't say anything about any of this. He might want to lock us up, too."

Mavice, Morna, and Glenda were just coming out of the doctor's office. Tincrowdor told them he would see them in a minute; he wanted a few words with the doctor. He entered and said, "Hi, Jack. Anything cooking on the grange?"

Croker was six-feet three-inches tall, almost too handsome, and looked like a Tarzan who had lately been eating too many bananas. He shook hands with Tincrowdor and said, in a slight English accent, "We can dispense with the private jokes."

"Sorry. Laughter is my defense," Tincrowdor said. "You must really be worried about Paul."

The door opened, and Morna entered. She said, "You gave me the high sign to come back alone, Jack. What's wrong?"

"Promise me you won't say anything to the family. Or to anybody," he said. He gestured at a microscope under which was a slide. "Take a look at that. You first, Morna, since you're a lab tech. Leo wouldn't know what he was seeing."

Morna bent over, made the necessary adjustments, looked for about ten seconds, and then said, "Lord!"

"What is it?" Leo said.

Morna straightened. "I don't know."

"Neither do I," Croker said. "I've been ransacking my books, and it's just as I suspected. There ain't no such thing."

"Like the giraffe," Leo said. "Let me look. I'm not as ignorant as you think."

A few minutes later, he straightened up. "I don't know what those other things are, the orange, red, lilac, deep blue, and purple-blue cells. But I do know that there aren't any organisms shaped like a brick with rounded ends and colored a bright yellow."

"They're not only in his blood; they're in other tissues, too," Croker said. "My tech found them while making a routine test. The things seem to be coated with a waxy substance which doesn't take a stain. I put some specimens in a blood agar culture, and they're thriving, though they're not multiplying. I stayed up all night running other tests. Eyre is a very healthy man, aside from a mental withdrawal. I don't know what to make of it, and to tell you the truth, I'm scared!

"That is why I had him put in isolation, and yet I don't want to alarm anybody. I've got no evidence that he's a danger to anybody. But he's swarming with something completely unknown. It's a hell of a situation, because there's no precedence to follow."

Morna burst into tears. Leo Tincrowdor said, "And if he recovers from his catatonia, there's nothing you can do to keep him here."

"Nothing legal," Croker said.

Morna snuffled, wiped her tears, blew her nose, and said, "Maybe it'll just pass away. Those things will disappear, and it'll be just another of those medical mysteries."

"I doubt it, Pollyanna," Tincrowdor said. "I think this is just the beginning."

"There's more," Croker said. "Epples, the nurse assigned to him, has a face deeply scarred with acne. Had, I should say. She went into his room to check on him, and when she came out, her face was as smooth and as soft as a baby's."

There was a long silence before Tincrowdor said, "You mean, you actually mean, that Paul Eyre performed a miracle? But he wasn't conscious! And—"

"I was staggered, but I am a scientist," Croker said. "Shortly after Epples, near hysteria, told me what happened, I noticed that a wart on my finger had disappeared. I remembered that I'd had it just before I examined Eyre . . ."

"Oh, come *on!*" Morna said.

"Yes, I know. But there's more. I've had to reprimand a male nurse, a sadistic apish-looking man named Backers, for unnecessary roughness a number of times. And I've suspected him, though I've had no proof, of outright cruelty in his treatment of some of the more obstreperous patients. I've been watching him for some time, and I would have fired him long ago if it weren't so hard to get help."

"Shortly after Epples had left Eyre and not knowing yet that her scars were gone, she returned to the room. She caught Backers sticking a needle in Eyre's thigh. He said later that he suspected Eyre of faking it, but he had no business being in the room or testing Eyre. Epples started to chew Backers out, but she didn't get a chance to say more than two words. Backers grabbed his heart and keeled over. Epples called me and then gave him mouth-to-mouth treatment until I arrived. I got his heart started with adrenalin. A half hour later, he was able to tell me what happened.

"Now Backers has no history of heart trouble, and the EKG I gave him indicated that his heart is normal. I—"

"Listen," Tincrowdor said, "are you telling me you think Eyre can both cure and kill? With thought projection?"

"I don't know how he does it or why. I'd have thought that Backer's attack was just a coincidence if it hadn't been for Epples' acne and my wart. I put two and two together and decided to try a little experiment. I felt foolish doing it, but a scientist rushes in where fools fear to tread. Or maybe it's the other way around.

"Anyway, I released some of my lab mosquitoes into Eyre's room. And behold, the six which settled on him expecting a free meal fell dead. Just keeled over, like Backers."

There was another long silence. Finally, Morna said, "But if he *can* cure people . . .?"

"Not *he*," Croker said. "I think those mysterious yellow microorganisms in his tissues are somehow responsible. I know it seems fantastic, but—"

"But if he can cure," Morna said, "how wonderful!"

"Yes," Leo said, "but if he can also kill, and I say *if*, since he'll have to be tested further before such a power can be admitted as possible, if, I say, he can kill anybody that threatens him, then . . ."

"Yes?" Croker said.

"Imagine what would happen if he were released. You can't let a man like that loose. Why, when I think of how often I've angered him! It'd be worse than uncaging a hungry tiger on Main Street."

"Exactly," Croker said. "And as long as he's in catatonia, he can't be released. Meanwhile, he is to be in a strict quarantine. After all, he may have a deadly disease. And if you repeat any of this to anybody else, including his family, I'll deny everything. Epples won't say anything, and Backers won't either. I've had to keep him on so I can control him, but he'll keep silent. Do you understand?"

"I understand that he might be here the rest of his life," Tincrowdor said. "For the good of humanity."

Part Two:
THE STAR-
TOUCHED

CHAPTER ONE

THE iron door with the monocle window swung inward. A small cage was shoved in, and a chain connected to it was pulled. The door of the cage rose. A large brown-gray male rat dashed out. The big door closed swiftly and silently.

The windowless room was ten by eight by twelve feet. Its white plaster walls were bare. A closed-circuit TV camera squatted on a bracket at the juncture of a wall and the ceiling. It pointed down at the only furniture: a bed, a chair, and a metal cabinet. The narrow bed held a man. Eyes closed, he lay on his back, his arms by his side, his feet pointing straight up. He was five feet six inches long, broad-shouldered, narrow-waisted, and slim. He was fifty-four years old and had brown hair untouched by gray, a high forehead, bushy brown eyebrows, a thick military-type mustache, and a chin like a ball, deeply indented in its middle. He wore only a hospital gown, His right arm and his left leg were chained to the metal frame of the bed.

The rat ran around the room, sniffing at the base of the walls, then clawed up the sheets of the bed to the man's left foot. It sniffed at the shackle around the ankle and began gnawing at the thick creamy stuff smeared on the shackle.

The cheese, mixed with flecks of crab-meat, disappeared rapidly. The rat touched the man's leg several times with its nose as if searching for more food. The man did not move his leg; his eyelids remained closed.

The rat ran along the man's leg and stopped on the man's stomach. When the man still did not move, the rat crept forward slowly, its nose twitching. It sprang forward at the daub of cheese mixed with meat on the man's face.

The rat never got to the face. It slumped and rolled off the man's body and fell by his neck. Its open mouth revealed that its teeth had been pulled.

The man behind the door turned pale, and he swore. He beckoned to a figure standing at the far end of the hall. A nurse, clothed from head to foot in white coveralls and gloves and a hood with a glass face mask, hurried to him. "Get the rat!" he said.

The nurse gave him a strange look and went inside. With gloved hands, she picked up the dead rat and put it into the cage and came back out of the room. The man locked the door and put the key in the pocket of his white laboratory coat.

"Take it to the lab."

He looked inside the room. The man in the bed had not moved. But it was evident to the watcher that something in the man had detected the danger and taken appropriate measures. And yet it was all impossible.

CHAPTER TWO

Leo Queequeg Tincrowdor, looking scared, came out of the woods. He had gone over almost every foot of the area. There were thorn tangles only rabbits could penetrate, and he had scratched his face and hands trying to get into them. His boots were wet for he had waded across the creek that bisected the woods, and mud streaked the sides of his jacket and pants. He had slipped while reaching for a branch to pull himself up a steep bank.

Of the yellow stuff that Eyre had reported, Tincrowdor had seen nothing. But the thing that had turned him pale and made him want to run out of the trees was the impression in the mud even the recent heavy rains had failed to obliterate. It looked innocuous enough. It was only an indentation of some hemispherical object that had been set upon a patch free of grass.

Eyre had told of seeing the thing in a dream, but Tincrowdor was convinced that Eyre was reporting an actual occurrence. He had driven down to the farm where Eyre had been hunting, and had heard the farmer's story of how Riley, Eyre's pointer, had run up onto the porch of the house and cowered under the glider. The farmer had not noticed the dog until he came home for lunch, when his wife told him of seeing the dog run panic-stricken across the fields toward the house. She thought that something had happened to Paul Eyre, but then she saw him standing near the edge of the woods. He seemed all right, so she supposed that the dog had lost its nerve over something and that Eyre would explain when he returned from his quail hunting. Eyre went into the woods and did not come out for several hours. When he did he tried to drag the dog out from under the glider. It leaped for Eyre's face and bit his hand, which Eyre had thrust in front of his face. Eyre tossed the dog over the porch railing and then, as it came after him again, killed it with a charge from his shotgun.

When Eyre told Tincrowdor about the dog, he had professed ignorance about why it had attacked him. Eyre had come home,

slept for a while, or so he said, and had had
a strange dream about his hunting of that
morning. In the dream, Riley had flushed
out two quail, and Eyre had shot at the lead
bird. Even as he fired, he realized that it
was not a quail but a flying saucer about
two feet in diameter. The thing had been hit
by the pellets from Eyre's gun and had
descended into the woods. Eyre had gone
after it but at the edge of the woods had
encountered a yellow mist. Some of the
mist had coagulated into drops, like a
golden-colored mercury.

Then, in his dream, he had seen the
saucer drop from a tree onto the ground.
He had followed it, had seen the rear parts
of a lioness disappear into the bush, and a
few moments later, the head and shoulders
of a naked woman. She was the loveliest
woman he had ever seen.

The following Monday morning, while
driving to work, Eyre had suddenly pulled
his car over to the side of the road. Fellow
workers in a car behind his had investi-
gated and found him in a complete mental
withdrawal. Mavice, his wife, had had him
taken to a nearby private sanitarium. His
condition was diagnosed as catatonia origi-
nating from causes unknown.

Tincrowdor and Eyre's son, Roger, had
searched through the cornfield along the
road where Eyre had stopped his car. They
had found some paw prints that Roger, a

zoology student, said were those of a large feline, a lion's or a tiger's. The big cat must have had wings, because its prints appeared suddenly between some rows about twenty yards inside the field and disappeared as suddenly about twenty feet deeper inside the field.

Tincrowdor had then gone to the sanitarium, where his friend and poker partner, Dr. Jack Croker, had shown him and Morna Tincrowdor some slides of Eyre's blood.

Four days later, Tincrowdor had decided that he would check out the woods in which Eyre had hunted. Now he knew that Eyre had been reporting, under the guise of a dream, reality.

Tincrowdor was a writer of science fiction, and as such he should have been pleased. A wounded flying saucer, golden haze flowing from the wound, a lovely sphinx, and strange yellow brick-shaped organisms in the tissues of the man who had hunted the saucer and the sphinx. These were the stuff of which science-fiction dreams were made.

Tincrowdor did not look pleased. He looked terrified.

CHAPTER THREE

Paul Eyre had been dreaming of a glittering green city at the far end of an enormous field of red flowers. His eyes opened. He had felt happy until then. He sat up, shocked. He remembered seeing the woman's face among the stalks of corn, the glimpse of the great tawny body beneath her torso, and his foot on the brake pedal. The car had slid to a stop on the shoulder of the road. He had put the gear into park and stared at her. She had smiled and waved a white arm at him. Her teeth were not human; they were sharp and widely separated, like a cat's, though they were even. He had begun shaking, and then he had fainted.

And here he was in a strange and bare room.

He started to get off the bed and became aware that an arm and leg were chained to the bed. "Hey, what's going on here?" he yelled. "What's going on?"

His ears drummed, and his heart jumped. He lay down again and stared at the single bright light, a bulb in the ceiling shielded by heavy wires. Then he saw the TV camera, like a one-eyed gargoyle squatting on a metal ledge. A few minutes later, the door opened. A woman shrouded in white cloth and glass entered. In one gloved hand, she held a hypodermic syringe.

The momentarily opened door had revealed, in the hall, a broad and heavy male face with thick black eyebrows, a broken nose, and thick lips.

"How are you, Mr. Eyre?" a muffled voice said from behind the glass plate. She stood at the foot of the bed as if she were waiting for permission to advance.

"Where am I? What's going on?"

"You're in the Adler Sanitarium. You've been in a catatonic state for four days. I'm Mrs. Epples, and I'm here to help you get well. I'd like to give you a shot. It's just to tranquilize you; it won't hurt you."

She was speaking so strangely, so unlike a nurse, he realized, because she was afraid of him. If he said no, she wasn't going to insist.

He felt weak, and his stomach rumbled. He was hungry and weak. His mouth felt as dry as an ostrich's feather.

"I don't want any shot," he said, "so forget it. Why am I chained to this bed? What are you doing in that getup? Do I have some disease?"

The woman looked up at the cold eye of the TV camera as if she expected to get some reassurance from it.

"So many questions at once," she said, and she laughed nervously. "You're chained to keep you from hurting yourself. We don't know if you have a disease or not, but your blood picture is strange. Until we know what those, uh, organisms are, we have to keep you in quarantine."

"My left arm and right leg are not chained," he said. "So what's to keep me from using them to hurt myself, if that's really what you're worried about? And what organisms are you talking about?"

"They're unknown," she said, ignoring his first comment.

"What if I have to relieve myself."

"There's a bedpan and toilet paper on the shelf in the stand." she said. "You can reach it."

"And how do I call you to take the pan away?"

"We'll know when you need someone," she said, glancing at the TV camera.

"You mean that someone'll be *watching* me?"

She shrank back, and said, "We don't

want you to hurt yourself."

"You have no right to keep me here!" he shouted. "I want out! Now!"

"I'll bring you your food," she said, and she left.

Eyre's rage moved along the spectrum from red to blue. He became frightened and confused. If he had awakened in a strait jacket, and the nurse had told him he had been crazy, he would have understood that. But everything in his situation was *wrong*. He was being held prisoner and lied to. He had no doubt that he was here because of what had happened in the woods—when?— five days ago. And the woman, Mrs. Epples, was afraid of him for some reason. Yet, he was supposed to have lain here in a—what was it?—a cata-something or other? Like a coma? What could he have done to scare her so? Or, was she telling the truth about his blood having some sort of strange germs?

All his life, he had been unable to just sit still and think unless he was figuring out some mechanical device. And then he needed paper and pencil to work out his ideas. He read only the newspapers and journals dealing with hunting or cars or motorboats, or technical books concerned with his type of work. He could sit for an hour or so watching TV or talking to friends, but then he became restless and had to be up and doing.

Or, perhaps not so much doing, he thought, as moving. He had to keep moving. Why?

It was the first time in his life he had ever asked himself that question. The first time he had asked himself anything about himself. And why was that?

It didn't take many brains to see that his feelings—Tincrowdor would say, his sensitivity—had been sharpened. Nor did it take much intelligence to connect this sharpening with the incident in the wood. Which might mean that the organisms in his blood were responsible. Which meant that they were beneficial. Or did it? Paul Eyre did not really like having improved insight. He was like a man who had spent his whole life building an impregnable castle only to find out that he himself was breaking down its walls.

This analogy made him even more ill at ease. He wasn't used to thinking in nonmechanical terms.

He took refuge in logic. If the organisms had caused changes in him of which he was aware, they had also caused changes of which he knew nothing. Otherwise, why would he be isolated and why would the nurse be so scared of him?

While he was pondering this, he fell asleep. When he awoke, he felt sure that he had been drugged. There were needle marks on his left arm, so many that he must have had some of them when he had first awakened. But he had been so disturbed then that he had not noticed them. Some of them, though, must have come from intravenous feeding. While he slept, he was nourished on a liquid diet.

What had made him drop off so suddenly? He looked around and presently found what he knew he would find. There was, in the shadow cast by the TV, the opening of a small pipe. An anesthetic gas had been expelled into the room to make him unconscious, and the nurse had come in after the gas had been dispelled and had given him a shot and set up the I.V. apparatus.

The gas alone was enough to keep him from escaping. They must really fear him if they thought he also had to be chained to the bed.

His feelings were not limited to fear and rage. Such precautions also made him feel important. And this was the first time in his life that he had felt, deep down, that he was of any significance to anybody.

He sat up and tested his strength against the chains. He was weak, but even if he had had his full power, he could not come near breaking the steel links. And even if he could, whoever was watching him through the TV would release the gas.

He lay down again and contemplated his situation. It was like life; you couldn't leave it until you died.

CHAPTER FOUR

Dr. Jack Croker and Leo Tincrowdor sat in Croker's office tearing each other and themselves apart.

"Mavice says that if you don't let her see Paul, she'll get him out of here," Tincrowdor said.

"She'd just be upset if she saw him," Croker said. "And I don't think it'd be wise for her to get anywhere near him. You know why. So why don't you talk her into leaving him in my care?"

"I can't tell her why it's so vital that he be isolated," Tincrowdor said. "And if she's not told, she won't see any reason not to move him elsewhere. Besides, what solid proof do you have that he is dangerous? None, none at all."

Croker could think of evidence. He regretted now telling Tincrowdor anything at all.

"What else has happened?" Tincrowdor said.

"What do you mean?" Croker said. He lit a cigarette to give himself time to think.

"You told me that your lab tech's face was badly scarred from adolescent acne. But after she took blood from Eyre, her face miraculously cleared up. And you said that Backers, a male nurse, had a heart attack while he was in the room with Paul. You were thinking of firing Backers because of his brutality, and you suspected that he was doing something to Paul when the heart attack occurred. It's obvious to anyone with imagination that you believe that those alien organisms have changed Paul, have given him strange powers. And it's obvious that you fear that those organisms might be infectious."

Croker bit his lip. If he told Tincrowdor that the organisms had disappeared, or at least were no longer detectible, then he would have lost one more reason for keeping Eyre. But he was not sure that they had all been excreted. There might be some in tissues unavailable until Eyre died. In his brain, for instance.

"We've collected about two million of the

yellow creatures in his urine and fecal matter," he said. "Boiling them in hot water doesn't kill them nor does depriving them of oxygen. About the only way they can be quickly destroyed is through burning. And that takes a minimum temperature of 1500 degrees Fahrenheit. It takes hours for the strongest acids to eat through the coating."

Tincrowdor said, "That alone should make you think they're of extraterrestrial origin."

He regretted saying this immediately. He hadn't told Croker about the paw print in the cornfield or the saucer print in the woods. If Croker really thought the yellow-brick things were from outer space, then he would be adamant about not releasing Eyre.

Nor could Tincrowdor blame him. Paul Eyre free could be a calamity, perhaps extinction, for humanity. But Eyre was a human being with certain inalienable rights. Never mind that most of his fellow Americans professed to believe the same but acted as if they didn't. He believed.

Still, he didn't want to die, along with everybody else, if Eyre really were a danger.

Yet, there were times in the velvet hours of the night, and the clanging minutes of noon, when he wondered if it wouldn't be a good thing if humanity were wiped out. For their own good, of course. Human beings suffered much, some more than others, but they all suffered. Death would put an end to their pain. It would also prevent the birth of more babies whose main inheritance would be pain. Tincrowdor had an obsession about babies. They were born good, he believed, though they had potentialities for evil. Society invariably insisted that they should grow up good, but provided the best and the most fertilizer for evil.

Croker, like most doctors, thought that this was the best of all possible worlds, which was to be expected. Their world gave doctors great respect and prestige and much wealth. It was natural for them to become angry with anything or anybody that might change things as they were. Yet, outside of the very poor, criminals, and policemen, they saw more of evil than anybody. But they fought against anything that might soften evil, just as they had fought against medical insurance until they suddenly saw that a good thing could be made out of it.

Croker was not, however, a typical specimen of his profession. He had some imagination. Otherwise he could not have been a member of the Baker Street Irregulars, the society that proceeds on the premise that Sherlock Holmes was a living person.

It was this imagination that made Croker connect things that his duller colleagues would have seen as entirely disparate. This same gift made him a danger to Eyre.

Tincrowdor was aware that Croker was aware and that Croker, like himself, was being stretched like a piece of bubble gum between his conscience and his duty. Or perhaps, Tincrowdor thought, they were each bubbles being blown up by the situation. If they didn't act soon, they would pop.

And the trouble with me, thought Tincrowdor, is that I'm not really concerned with Paul Eyre as an individual human being. I don't even like Eyre. He'd be better off dead and so would his family. But then, come to think of it, so would I. So why am I interfering? Especially when logic says that the fate of one miserable human being is nothing compared to that of the fate of all humanity.

For one thing, if Eyre were done away with, the case might be closed forever. That this might break off forever any contact with extraterrestrials alarmed him. Besides, like most science-fiction writers, he secretly hoped for vast cataclysms, end-of-the-world invasions from outer space, anything that would polish off most of mankind. Among the survivors would be himself, of course. And this little band, having learned its lesson, would then make a paradise of earth.

In his more light-filled moments he

laughed at this fantasy. The survivors wouldn't do a bit better than their predecessors.

Croker, who had been silent, said, "How about a drink, Leo?"

"Drink dims the conscious and illuminates the unconscious," Tincrowdor said, "Yes, I'll have one. Or several."

Croker brought out a fifth of Weller's Special Reserve, and the two silently toasted their thoughts.

Tincrowdor asked for another three fingers and said, 'If you murder Eyre, you might have to kill me, too. Not to mention Morna. You wouldn't have enough guts to do that."

"I could kill Eyre and then myself," Croker said cheerfully.

Tincrowdor laughed, but he was taken aback. "You've got too much curiosity to do that," he said. "You'd want to know what those yellow things are and where they came from."

"You'd better tell me all you know," Croker said. "I had thought that the organisms were mutations, though I didn't really believe that."

"You're less hidebound and more perceptive than I thought," Tincrowdor said. "O.K. I'll tell you everything."

Croker listened without interrupting except to request more detailed description of several events. Then he said, "Let me tell you about the rat I released in Eyre's room."

When Croker was finished, Tincrowdor poured himself another drink. Croker looked disapproving but said nothing. He had once shown the writer the brain and liver of a skid-row bum. Tincrowdor had quit drinking for three months. When he started again, he drank as if he were trying to make up for the lost time.

Tincrowdor sat down and said, "Even if Paul isn't carrying a contagious disease, he's a menace. He can kill anything he thinks is dangerous. Or, maybe anytime he gets angry. And he gets angry a lot."

He downed half his drink and said, "So that should make your course of action—and mine—apparent. You can't loose *that* on the world."

"And what will *you* do?" Croker said.

"My God, here are two intelligent and compassionate people discussing murder!" Tincrowdor said.

"I didn't mean that," Croker said. "I was thinking of keeping him locked up, as if he were a sort of Man in the Iron Mask. But I don't know if that is possible. In the first place, a fake death would have to be arranged, but that would lead to almost insuperable complications and connivery. He'd have to seem to have died in a fire, so the body would be unrecognizable. I'd have to supply a body so it'd be a closed-coffin funeral. I couldn't keep him here, because somebody might talk. I'd have to arrange for his transportation elsewhere, and I'd have to pay for his keep. And the first time he got angry or thought he was menaced, he'd kill. And that would cause trouble wherever he'd be."

"And if it all came out, you'd go to jail. And I'd be an accessory before, during, and after the fact. And, to tell you the truth, I don't have the guts to be your accomplice.

"Why'd you tell me anything in the first place?" Tincrowdor said. "Is it because you wanted someone to share the guilt?"

"Perhaps I thought that if anyone else knew about it, I'd not be able to do anything," Croker said.

"And you could release him with a clear conscience? Your hands'd be tied?"

"Perhaps. But that's out. I can't release him."

He leaned toward Tincrowdor and said, "If his family could be made aware of all the facts, they just might agree to keep him here. It might not be forever, because he may lose this power to kill by thought or however he does it. After all, the organisms have gone. Perhaps the power will, too."

"You don't know his family. Maybe his son and daughter would go along, because they're educated enough and have imagination enough to extrapolate from the situation. But Mavice? Never! She'd think we were crazy with all this talk of flying saucers and yellow stuff and killing by invisible means. The story would be out in no time. She would tell her brothers, who are also unimaginative clods. Not that they'd worry much about Paul. They don't like him. But they'd want to help their sister. She's the baby of their family, and they'd hear about it from her all right."

"Yeah," Croker said. "How'd you ever get to know the Eyres? They're certainly not the type you'd be friends with."

"Morna and Mavice were high-school buddies. Mavice stood by Morna when she was being ostracized by her other friends because of some lying story a boy was telling about her. They have been good friends ever since. Despite the disparity in their education and attitudes—Morna's a liberal, as you know, and Mavice's a flaming reactionary—they managed to get along fine. I had a little affair with Mavice myself, back in the days when I was young and horny and a fine female body meant more to me than a fine female brain."

"How you ever stood that screeching voice, I'll never understand," Croker said. "But that's neither here nor there. What if Mavice were told a story that doesn't quite fit the facts?"

"I don't know how you could do it and still not be exposed."

Croker erupted from his chair spilling

whiskey over his pants. "Well, something has to be done and soon!"

There was a knock on the door, and Croker said, "Who is it?"

"It's Mrs. Epples. May I come in?"

Croker opened the door. Mrs. Epples, looking past him, said, "I wanted to speak to you alone, Doctor."

Croker went out into the hall and shut the door. Tincrowdor looked at the fifth and decided not to have any more. A minute later, Croker entered. He looked pale.

"Eyre's dead!"

Tincrowdor opened his mouth, but Croker held up his hand.

"I know what you're thinking, but it's not true, so help me God. Eyre died of natural causes. At least, *I* didn't have anything to do with it."

CHAPTER FIVE

Paul Eyre awoke naked on something cold and hard. A scalpel was poised above him and beyond a face, its lower half hidden by a gauze mask. Above the men there glared a hard bright light.

The man's eyes widened, the scalpel jerked away, and he cried, "No! No!"

Eyre rolled off the stone and onto the floor. Though his legs and arms gave way to weakness, he crawled away toward the closed door. Something hard struck the marble floor. The metallic sound was succeeded a second later by the thump of a heavy body.

A few feet from the door, Eyre collapsed. He lay breathing heavily for awhile, knowing somehow that the immediate danger had passed. But out there, beyond the door, and not far away, were other dangers. They were walking up and down the corridors, intent on their business. At least two were thinking about him also.

Their thoughts were neither verbal or iconic. They blew through the door as thin susurruses from two far-off oceans. They lapped around him as the last waves of the sea would roll out on the beach and splash his feet.

As he sat up, he caught another element in the faint whisperings. It identified the sex of the thinkers.

He reached up, grabbed the edge of the stone table, and pulled himself up. Eyre walked around the table, leaning on it, and then got down on his knees to examine the man on the floor. His eyes were open and glazed, his skin was bluish, and he had no pulse. Something, probably a heart attack, had struck him down just as he was about to kill Eyre. But why had he wanted to murder Eyre and to dissect him?

He looked around the room and found nothing with which to clothe himself. The man's clothes wouldn't fit him, but if he had to, he would put them on. He couldn't stay naked. He had to get to a telephone and call the police, but if he went out into the corridor, he'd be seen at once. And there must be others in this plot to kill him. This man wouldn't have been acting alone.

Or would he?

He was confused and weak from lack of data as well as hunger. And being naked made him feel guilty, as if he had actually committed some crime that had justified the dead man's trying to kill him. First, he'd get some clothes and then he would get out.

He walked slowly to the door and opened it. The corridor was empty except for a very old man shuffling toward him. He wore slippers, pants, a shirt, and an old frayed bathrobe. He was about Eyre's size. His heart beating hard, Eyre waited until the old man was opposite him. He reached out an arm, grabbed the man by his sleeve, and yanked him inside. He disliked using violence on him, yet at the same time he felt angry at him. An image of his own father, aged beyond his years, his mouth hanging open, drooling, passed before him. He hated old people, he realized, and he hated them because they prefigured his own fate.

The hate was good in one way. It gave him the strength to do what was needed. Fortunately, the old man was paralyzed with fright and did not fight. If he had, he might have caused Eyre considerable trouble, Eyre was so weak.

The old man squawked before Eyre could get a hand over the toothless mouth. The door banged shut. The old man rolled his eyes and went limp. Eyre eased him down and began to undress him. At least, the old man didn't stink from lack of bathing. But Eyre couldn't bring himself to put on the stained shorts. Evidently the old man had imperfect control over his bladder.

When Eyre had finished dressing, he looked at the old man, who was still unconscious but breathing. And what would the fellow do when he awoke? He'd arouse everybody, and the hunt would be on. And when Eyre did get hold of the police, what then? Wouldn't the old man be able to charge Eyre with assault and the theft of his clothes? But surely the police would understand the necessity of this.

He had no time to consider the consequences of what he was doing. He had to get out and away.

He put the scalpel in the pocket of the bathrobe and stepped out into the hall. As he walked down the hall, he realized that he was not wearing his glasses. In fact, now that he thought back on it, he hadn't had them when he had awakened in that room. Yet, he had seen perfectly.

This frightened him for a moment but before he reached the end of the hall he felt reassured. Whatever was going on, it wasn't entirely malignant.

At the corner, he thought of stopping to reconnoiter. But it would be better to act as if he belonged here, so he shuffled to his right. He was in another hall, and at once he saw that he should have gone to his left. Ahead of him was a desk behind which sat a nurse, and beyond her another hall at right angles to his. And a man Eyre recognized was walking in it. His profile was that of the apish man Eyre had seen the last time Mrs. Epples had entered the room in which he had been confined.

He repressed the impulse to wheel and go in the opposite direction. A quick movement might attract the man's eye. The male nurse passed on, and Eyre stopped, felt in his pockets as if he had suddenly discovered he'd left something in his room, and then started to turn back. The nurse looked up and saw him.

"What can I do for you?" she said, sharply.

"Nothing," he said. "I forgot my cigarettes."

She stood up and said, "I don't believe I know you. Are you sure you're on the right floor?"

"I was admitted last night," he said and walked away. At the end of the corridor two doors opened onto a balcony. Through their windows he could see across a brightly lit court. He was on the first story.

"Just a minute!" the woman said. "I don't see any new names of the list!"

"Look closer!" he called back and then was trying the handles of the doors. They were locked, and he was not strong enough to break them open with his body. He went on down the hall to his left, ignoring the demands of the nurse that he come back. As soon as he was out of sight, he kicked off the slippers and ran as fast as he could, which was not swiftly, toward the door at its end. It was barred and locked, too. He turned and pushed open the door nearest him and entered. The bed was empty. The door to the bathroom was closed, and inside someone was flushing the toilet. On the bureau near the window were jars and tubes and boxes of ointments and powders.

The windows could be swung open inward, but the bars would prevent anything but air or messages from getting out.

He put his ear to the bathroom door. Despite the rush of water splashing in the washbowl, he could hear the voices in the hall. One was Mrs. Epples'.

"If you do see him, don't go near him, for God's sake!"

"Why not?" a woman said.

"Because he. . . ."

The voices trailed off as his pursuers presumably went down the hall to their left.

He opened the door and looked out. Mrs. Epples and another nurse were walking away from him. At the middle of the other hall, the apish male nurse was opening the door to a room. He was working his way down the hall, and soon would be opening the door behind which Eyre stood.

The water was no longer splashing. The woman would be coming out in a minute. He withdrew his head from the hall, tried to estimate the time it would take for the nurse to open the next door, and stepped out into the hall. Another door down the hall was open, and a nurse was looking into the room. Eyre was around the corner and out of sight; the two nurses had disappeared. He was congratulating himself when Mrs. Epples came out of a room four doors from him. He halted, and she screamed.

Before he could go on, she had dodged back into the room and slammed the door. Behind him he heard a shout and the slap of shoes on the floor.

Eyre ran again. There was another shout. He glanced over his shoulder and saw the apish man standing by the corner. Evidently he had no intentioin of pursuing him any further.

A door opened ahead of him and a thin young man with tousled hair and wild eyes looked out, but when he saw Eyre he cowered against the bed. Eyre did not believe that he was frightened because he knew anything about him. The young man would have been frightened by any stranger.

Eyre said nothing. He went to the closet, opened it, and took out a pair of hush puppies and a jacket. In the bureau drawer he found a wallet and removed a ten-dollar bill, a five, four ones, and some change.

"I'll pay you back later," he said.

The young man shivered and his teeth chattered.

Paul Eyre stepped out of the room just as Mrs. Epples and the apish male nurse came around a corner. They halted, stared at him, and fled.

They were afraid of him, no doubt, but they must have gone for help. However, if everybody was as scared as those two, nobody was going to stop him. Not unless they shot at him from a distance.

Two minutes later, he walked out of the Adler Sanitarium. Only a security guard, a sixty-year-old-man, stood between Eyre and freedom. He stepped aside as Eyre approached him because Mrs. Epples was screaming at him from the front entrance.

"Don't use your gun! Let him go! The police will take care of him!"

This startled Eyre. Why would *they* bring in the police? He was the one who had been held prisoner and whom they, or at least some of them, had tried to kill. Or, did they have some good reason for having held him? Was he—he felt cold at the thought—was he carrying some dreadful disease? Had he been infected by that yellow stuff?

If this were so, why hadn't he been told?

He would have cooperated to the fullest.

There were about thirty cars in the parking lot. Some of them had unlocked doors, but none of them had keys in the ignition locks. He didn't want to take the time to crosswire one, so he started walking down the road. As soon as he was out of sight of the sanitarium, he turned right into the woods. The Illinois River lay a mile and a half away, and a half mile up its bank was a refuge.

CHAPTER SIX

The cottage belonged to a friend who had invited the Eyre family Saturday afternoons for boating and water-skiing and a big meal at night. They would sleep in the two extra rooms, get up for a big breakfast about ten, go to a nearby church, and spend the afternoon on the river. Eyre paid for these weekends by repairing Gardner's boat motors or helping him paint his boats.

The season was over, and the house was shut up. Eyre knew that it held canned foods and blankets. He could hide out there while he tried to find out what was happening to him.

The cottage was about twenty yards from the river and was isolated from the neighboring houses by thick woods on each side. He crouched in the thick bushes behind a big tree while the moon rose.

About two hours after he had hidden, car lights probed down the narrow dirt road leading to the cottage. Shivering, he lay down flat on the cold ground in a little hollow behind the bush. When the lights had passed him, he raised his head. Two cars were parked in the moonlit area before the house. Men in the uniforms of the county police were tramping around the house with flashlights. Presently two went in, and their flashlights speared the darkness within. After ten minutes, the two came out. One of them said, "There's no sign he's been here."

"Yeah, but he might come here later."

One talked over the radio for a minute, then called to the others. "The sheriff said to watch the Y-fork for an hour."

The cars drove away. Eyre stayed where he was. A half-hour later a patrol car, its lights off, rolled into the open area before the house. Two men got out quietly, tried the locks, and cast their flashlight beams through the windows. A few minutes later, they got into the car and drove off.

Eyre waited until three in the morning before entering the house. An extra key was hidden in a stump by the woodpile. Whoever had told the police about this cottage—he suspected Mavice—had forgotten about the key. The moonlight coming in the windows and his knowledge of the place enabled him to locate a bottle of distilled water, a box of powdered milk, and cans of fruit and meat. The water and gas were shut off, so he could not cook, and he had to go outside to relieve himself.

At three thirty, he crawled onto the unsheeted mattress under a pile of blankets. He fell asleep at once but dreamed of flying saucers, yellow bricks, and a green city far off across a red field. He felt a great longing for the city, an over-whelming homesickness. He awoke with the tears only half-dried.

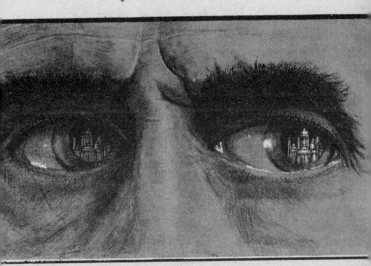

CHAPTER SEVEN

Half an hour after dawn, carrying two blankets, a can that he had filled with water, two opened cans of food, and a sack of garbage, he went back to his hiding place. He fell asleep. Two hours later he was awakened by noises from the house. A car with two county officers was parked out front. He was glad that he had replaced the key in the stump, for an officer was looking inside the stump. Somebody had recalled that it was there. Was it Mavice who had betrayed him? Or one of the kids? Gardner must have given a key to the police, but somebody in Eyre's family had told the police about the cottage. They would not have known about Gardner otherwise.

An officer came out of the house and called to the other.

"Everything's just as we left it."

Fortunately, they had not counted the blankets.

A moment later, the sound of a motor announced another car. His ear identified it as a Porsche, and thus he was not overly surprised when Tincrowdor drove up. What was he doing here?

Tincrowdor got out and talked to the officers, but they spoke too softly for Eyre to hear what they were saying. Several times, Tincrowdor looked out at the woods, and once he looked directly at Eyre but could not see him, of course. Eyre hoped that he wasn't going to suggest to the police that they search the woods.

The policeman got into the car, and Tincrowdor started toward his. As he passed the stump, he dropped something into its open end.

Eyre waited for a half-hour and went to the stump. The key still dangled on a thick cord from a nail driven into the interior wall. Below it lay an old and frayed wallet. He opened it and found a folded letter in it.

Paul,

I'm taking a chance that you may come here and find this. The police don't know I'm doing this, but if they find this, there's nothing they can do about it. I'm only trying to get you to surrender yourself. But please don't tear this up at this point. Read on, because it is vitally important that you do. And when I say *vitally,* I am not exaggerating. It's vital not only for you but possibly for the world itself that you make yourself available at once for study. Study by scientists.

Roger and I found evidence that you were lying when you said you'd dreamed. We know that it must have been reality but that you were afraid you'd be thought crazy if you reported it as reality. And Croker, poor dead Croker, found evidence that you were infected with a completely unknown organism.

It's evident that these things have made some changes in your body. And in your mind. Mrs. Epples had a very badly scarred face from adolescent acne. The scars disappeared after she assisted in getting you to bed in the sanitarium. A male nurse, Backers, suffered a heart attack when he apparently manhandled you. He is a rather brutal person and was not discharged only because help is hard to get at Adler's. No wonder, considering its' very low pay scale.

It's obvious that you have powers that nobody else has ever had. Except in science-fiction stories. Or, possibly, some people in the past have had them—Jesus, Faustus, some others, maybe some so-called witch doctors of so-called primitive peoples.

I wouldn't advise you to try walking on the surface of the Illinois. But you can hurt, you can *kill,* and you can *heal.* I don't mean that you can do this consciously. At least not yet. But when you, or your unconscious, or whatever, feels threatened, it reacts violently. By what means, I don't know. I'd guess, by mental means. Definitions or analyses don't matter just now.

You have powers for good and evil. You struck down Croker in, I presume, a moment of panic. Yet, Croker was not trying to kill you. He thought you were dead. You were kept prisoner in that room, and your unconscious, or whatever, took the only means of getting you out of that room. At least, I'm presuming you didn't do it consciously. Your body became, as far as Croker could tell, dead. But you came out of that fake-death state when you were about to be dissected. And Croker paid the price for trying to keep your *condition* a secret.

It's a good thing I'm squeamish and wasn't present to watch the dissection. I went home and so was spared. The old man whose clothes you took seemed to have had a mild heart attack. Apparently you, or whatever, didn't feel that he was an important threat. He died a few hours later, anyway. His old heart couldn't take the minor injury you gave it.

I'm asking you to turn yourself in, Paul.

You should voluntarily allow yourself to be locked up, for awhile, at least. You won't be charged with murder or manslaughter, because you couldn't help the deaths. But if you persist in hiding, in running away, you'll be killing more people, and, eventually, you'll be killed.

At the moment, there is very little evidence that your story is true. Croker hid the slides of your blood and his reports on you. We can't find them. Not yet. But Epples and Backers saw the experiment with the rat. You were in an unconscious state, Paul, but you killed a rat that had been released in your room and tried to bite you. It couldn't because its teeth had been removed. You killed it without moving a muscle.

If you give yourself up, the scientists can test you and they'll have to believe what they see. They won't want to, but they'll have to. And then they'll have to believe that an extraterrestrial of some sort, mechanical or biological, has landed on earth. This knowledge they will have to keep to themselves while a quiet search for the extee is conducted. If the news got out, the panic would be terrible.

I won't lie to you, Paul. If the world found out that you were a possible source of infection, you'd be in grave danger. But that's why you need to be kept in a place that is heavily guarded. While you're running around loose, the news might get out, and every man's hand would be against you.

Why do I take the chance that the police may find this letter and so bring about the very situation I've described? Because the situation demands that I take this chance. You are the most important person in the world, Paul. The most important.

You must give yourself up and let events fall where they may.

You know my phone number. Call me and I'll make arrangements to meet you and have you given a safe conduct.

Leo

CHAPTER EIGHT

Paul Eyre sat in his daughter Glenda's car in the parking lot of Busiris Central High School. It had taken him three hours to settle down his heart and thoughts. By the end of that time he had half-convinced himself that he was indeed the danger Tincrowdor had said he was. He still did not intend to give himself up; at least, not yet. He had little imagination but the letter had shown him what could happen to him. He might be kept the rest of his life in a hospital room. He might be killed by some fanatic who wanted to rid the world of the threat to it he represented. All the guards and precautions that could be imagined would not be enough to make him safe from determined men.

And yet, he wanted to do his duty. Duty demanded that he sacrifice himself for the sake of the world. He could be a walking bomb a thousand times more fatal than a dozen H-bombs.

He did not really feel that he was. He felt lonely and helpless and very scared. He felt like a leper. He felt self-pity. Why had this horrible thing happened to *him*, of all people? What had he done to deserve it? He wasn't a wicked person. He had his faults, though at the moment he couldn't think of any, but they weren't great enough for him to be singled out for a singular punishment. All he had wanted to do was to keep working at Trackless and on his own little business, to enjoy a beer now and then, to go fishing and hunting, to retire someday and spend his remaining years camping, fishing, and hunting. And work on some gadget that would make him rich and famous.

That was all he wanted.

Now, he thought, he knew what the deer and the rabbits felt like when he had been after them. Not that he regretted shooting them. They were beasts of the field, provided by God for his pleasure and good. He had none of that false sentimentality that permitted some to be horrified by the deaths of gentle-eyed and harmless deer, while they thought nothing of slaughter of gentle-eyed and harmless cattle and sheep for their tables. He didn't see them confining themselves to nuts, carrots, and apples.

Nevertheless, as he had made his way through the woods and the city to this parking lot, he had experienced the same horror that the deer must have experienced.

Busiris, a city of 150,000 population, stretched six miles along the western shores of the Illinois. It also covered the three bluffs inland for a distance of five miles. He had walked through the forests and by the farms and the few industries on its northern side, ascended the bluff through some woods, and walked through the outlying areas. He had to cross some of the major roads, and the closer he got to the high school, the more chance he had of being recognized. But he had shaved off his mustache in the cottage, and he was not wearing his glasses.

Using a screwdriver taken from the cottage, Eyre pried open the front left window of Glenda's car. Reaching in with the other, he brought up the lock on the inside of the door. A moment later, he had crosswired the car and had the motor running. If he were spotted by a patrol car, he would at least try to get away in her Impala.

Three thirty came. The big building spewed forth students. Over two-thirds of the cars had left the lot when Glenda appeared. She had a beautiful though thin face and long black hair. Yet, she was a pitiful figure. She would have been five feet eight inches tall if her back had been an exclamation mark instead of an interrogative. Her legs seemed as thin as the back of a cigarette package. One leg was several inches shorter than the other. She walked with a motion suggestive of a sick snake.

Glenda was a living reproach to her father, though he had only recently recognized it. He had been disappointed when she was born because he had wanted another son. Girls were useless; they demanded special care, became a worry when they were pubescent, and beyond helping their mothers when they got older, couldn't pay their way in his household. Paul Eyre had, however, determined that his daughter was going to be as much like a boy as possible. He had taught her how to repair cars and outboard motors, to do carpentry and electrical work, and to hunt and fish. At least, when she got married, she wasn't going to be a drag like Mavice. Mavice had refused to learn enough to help him in his business. And when she reluctantly went along on his outdoor trips, she griped about the cooking, the boredom and the discomforts.

When Glenda was ten, she had gone with him and Roger to Wisconsin on a fishing

trip. She had not been feeling well for
several days and had objected to going.
Mavice had objected, too. He had stormed
at both of them until they subsided. On
reaching the little lake, Glenda had become
too sick to leave the tent. Eyre had ignored
all except her most basic demands and had,
in fact, been angry because he thought she
was malingering. The second day, Glenda
had a high fever and was only conscious
now and then. Finally realizing the serious-
ness of the situation, he had bundled her
into a car and driven all night back to
Busiris.

Glenda had almost died of infantile paral-
ysis. And she would always be a cripple.

She had never said anything to him about
his forcing her to go on the trip. Mavice,
however, had more than made up for
Glenda's silence. How many times, when
they were quarreling, had Mavice thrown
this up to him?

Now, watching her hobble bent-backed
across the lot, he felt sick. And he
understood why her mere presence had
made him so angry, why he had longed for
the day she would go off to college. Deep
down, he knew that it was his selfishness
and stupidity that had wrecked her. He had
refused to admit that knowledge to his
consciousness, but it had nevertheless
disturbed him.

He also saw for the first time that Mavice

was to blame, too. Why hadn't she held out against him? No matter how he had ranted, she should have refused to let him take an obviously sick child on such a trip.

Both of them were guilty. Both had refused to admit their guilt. The only difference now was that Mavice was still blind, and something had suddenly and painfully opened his eyes.

He knew what that something was. The strange organisms in his body had worked a change in him.

CHAPTER NINE

Glenda, seeing him in the driver's seat, stopped. Her pale face became even whiter. Then she came around the side of the car and got in beside him. Tears ran down her cheek.

"What are you doing here, Dad?"

He refrained from telling her that she was his second choice. Busiris College was too far away and too well patrolled for him to try to see Roger.

He told her all that had happened and described Tincrowdor's letter. Glenda looked stunned.

"I didn't want to phone Leo because the police might've tapped his wires," he said. "I want you to get to his house and arrange for him to be in the phone booth near the downtown public library. I'll call him from another booth."

"I just can't believe all this!" Glenda said. "It's too fantastic!"

"I'm not crazy, and Leo will tell you so," he said. "The world has enough problems, more than it can handle, as everybody, including God, knows. But now, in the past few days, it has two new problems. And both make all past problems look simple. One is that saucer creature. The other is me. I can turn myself in and give the world a chance to solve the dilemma I represent. But what's going to prevent the saucer thing from infecting other people? Nothing, nobody, is going to be able to do anything about that. Except me."

"What do you mean?" she said. She leaned over and placed a hand on his arm. He moved it away, feeling that he might be contagious.

"I mean that there's something of the saucer thing in me. It's changed me, is still changing me. I'm part saucer thing myself. Otherwise, why would I have those dreams of that green city and the longing for it? You see before you a man who's still your father but not your father. Half-human. Or, maybe I was only half-human before and it's making me more human. I don't know. Anyway, it takes a thief to catch a thief, and I'm the only one who can catch the saucer thing. That's because I'm part saucer thing, and the saucer thing herself is dogging me. Why, I don't know. There's so much I don't know. But I'm convinced that only I can trap her. Which is why I'm not going to turn myself in. But I need help to stay out of the hands of the police. That's why I want to talk to Tincrowdor. Maybe he'll help me."

"Dad," Glenda said in a choked voice. "I'm sick!"

She fell against him, and even through his shirt he could feel the heat from her face. He pushed her back so that she sat up as straight as she ever would be able to. Her head hung forward, mouth open; she breathed as if a rusty windmill was in her throat.

"I'm not *angry* with you, Glenda!" he cried. "My God, I love you!"

CHAPTER TEN

Once, he had deserted her when she had been sick. There had been no excuse for what he had done. Now, if he deserted her, he would have an excuse. He couldn't let himself be caught. And logic certainly told him to leave her. He could phone in to the hospital and then take off. Glenda would be taken care of, and he would be safe.

He thought for sixty seconds or so and then drove out of the lot and headed toward the Methodist Hospital. Glenda probably needed to get to a hospital as swiftly as possible, and he would not be responsible for even a second's delay.

He drove as fast as he could, passing three stop signs and two red lights. His car

121

pulled up at the emergency entrance four minutes later. After running inside and telling the nurse at the admittance desk, he went to the public phone down the hall. He dialed his home number but hung up after the phone had rung twenty times. Then he dialed Tincrowdor's number. Morna answered.

He told her to shut up and listen while he explained the situation.

"You get Mavice and Roger down here and take care of things," he said, "And tell Leo I'll be getting in touch with him. 'Bye!"

He walked down the hall away from the emergency room. He heard the nurse calling after him but did not look back. A minute later, he went out by the main exit, past the policeman standing guard there. He strode up the slope along the hospital, cut over to a side street that led to Main Street, and took a bus. Two blocks from his house, he got off at Sheridan and Lux. He phoned the hospital and asked for Mavice Eyre, the mother of the girl who had just been brought in. He waited for two minutes before Mavice answered, then hung up and walked to his house, hoping that Roger would not be there.

He saw no one who knew him until he got to his house. Across the street was the three-storied nursing home filled with old people who had often seen him come and go and watched him when he worked on cars and boats in his driveway. About eight of them, mostly old ladies, were sunning themselves on the side porch as he went up the driveway to the rear of his house. They looked curiously at him but none waved. Apparently, his strange clothes and lack of spectacles and mustache had deceived them.

Under a washbowl on a stand by the rear door was a key. Fifteen minutes later, he left his house. He was dressed in his own clothes and carried a wallet with fifty dollars and a shotgun and thirty shells. He got into Roger's car; its motor was still warm. Evidently Roger had gotten home just in time to drive his mother to the hospital in her car.

Paul Eyre had no specific place in mind to go. He would drive out of the city, abandon the car, and walk to one of the riverside cottages deserted for the season. There he would wait as long as he was left alone.

It didn't matter where he was. Sooner or later, the saucer thing in its saucer form, or in that of the sphinx, would show up. And then he would destroy it. Or, it would destroy him.

As he got to the end of his street, he saw a patrol car pull across it, blocking his car. He slammed on the brakes, backed with a squeal of tires into a driveway, and raced away. The rear-view mirror showed him the police car backing up so it could swing around.

When he looked again, he saw another black-and-white car, its red lights flashing, pull around the corner ahead of him.

He put the car into neutral, opened the door, and fell out of it while it was still moving. He ran for the old folks' home, the sanctuary of senior citizens, the elephants' graveyard. The old ladies on the front porch screamed. One stood in his path. Rage flashed through him. The woman fell on her face. Shouts of male voices tore at him, and as he went through the door into a huge dining room, he heard a shot. A warning fired into the air—he hoped.

He crossed a big room into a smaller one, went past that through a kitchen, and out the door. He vaulted over a fence with an agility he did not know he possessed. But he had forgotten about the savage police dog the Hunters kept. Though it was chained, it had enough leash to get at him. It sprang at him and dropped upon the ground and lay still, its tongue hanging out, its eyes glazing.

He stopped and turned toward the big house, his arms up in the air. If he kept on running, he would kill half the world, and he could not endure that thought. He would surrender now, and if the police shot him because they were afraid to let him stay alive, so much the better. That would solve many problems.

The police, of course, did not shoot. They had not been told how dangerous he was, nor did they know then that he had left three old women dead behind him. Even if they had, they would have thought that the excitement was too much for the aged hearts.

That is exactly what the few authorities who knew the truth allowed the police and the public to think. He was not brought to trial on any charge but was declared to have been examined by psychiatrists and found insane.

Eyre did not argue with the decision. Nor did he tell his keepers about the incident, three nights after being locked up, when he had awakened and looked out of the window. Outlined in its frame was a saucer shape. It hovered for a few seconds and then flashed upward out of sight. Eyre felt that it—she—was watching over him because he was her only living offspring. Or, something inside him was.

CHAPTER ELEVEN

Six months passed without his seeing a human being in the flesh. From time to time he awoke knowing that a gas had put him to sleep and samples of his tissues had been taken from him. Once, he awoke with an x-ray photo on the table beside him. The TV had come to life then, and Dr. Polar's image had told him what the x-ray meant. It was of his brain, and the arrow drawn on it pointed to a tiny spot in his cerebellum, the "hind brain." This was something that had been detected by radioactive tracing. It might be a tumor, but Dr. Polar did not think it was. Its shape was too much like a brick's. Dr. Polar admitted that he would like to operate to extract it. But he was afraid that the surgeon would drop dead before the knife could make its first cut.

"Apparently, *it* doesn't object to our taking tissue samples or doing certain other experiments," Polar said. "These don't threaten you, or it, I should say."

Eyre asked about *its* nature but was told that Polar and his colleagues didn't even have any theories about it. Eyre then asked if Polar planned to kill him so he could dissect him. Polar did not answer.

He also asked a number of times about Glenda. Each time, he was told that she was alive and doing well. That was all he could, or would, be told.

On the first day of the seventh month, as Eyre paced back and forth, the door to his room opened. Glenda walked in, and the door was quickly shut and locked.

Eyre was so overwhelmed that he had to sit down in his chair. Glenda stood tall and straight, her breasts were no longer just little buds, and her legs were even and shapely. She smiled at him and then broke into tears and ran to him. He cried, too, though at one time he would have thought it unmanly to do so.

"I almost died," she said, after she had left his arms. "My bones got soft. The doctors said nothing like this had ever happened before. They said the calcium was semi-dissolved. The bones were like rubber at first and then like a hard jelly.

They kept me in a kind of bath-bed; I floated in water while they put braces and molds around me to straighten me out. After a few weeks, the bones began to get hard again. It took two months for them to become completely hard, and it was so long, so very long, and so frightening! But look at me now!"

Eyre was happy for a long time. But when Glenda said that he wasn't going to be freed, he became angry.

"Why not? I can do great good, more good than anybody has ever done before!"

"Dad, they can't let you go. Everytime you got mad at someone, you'd kill him. Besides. . . ."

"Well, what is it?" he said. He hoped he wouldn't be getting angry with her. Maybe he should tell her to get out now.

"We're all in prison here!" she said, and she began to cry.

Though there was no reason to ask why, he did so. The authorities, whoever they were, had locked up not only his family but the two Tincrowdors, Mrs. Epples, and Backers in this place. They were well treated and given everything they wanted except their freedom.

"But what about our friends and relatives?"

"They've been told we are all being treated for a rare contagious disease. I don't know how long they're going to believe that, but I think some sort of indirect pressure is being put on them. They're not to say anything about this to anybody else. We get letters, and we can write letters. But they're censored. We've had to rewrite some of them."

Eyre was in a rage for two days and a funk for three. The sixth day, Dr. Polar appeared on the TV screen. He waited until Eyre had quit storming at him and then said, "It's not as bad as it seems to you, Paul. There may be a way out for all of us. I want you to go to the door now. The view-window will be opened for a minute. I want you to just look through it. That's all."

Since there was no reason to refuse, Eyre did so. He saw only a baby, about a year old, lying on a bed. The baby had a wasted face and very thin arms and legs and was obviously dying. Eyre felt pity for it.

Then the window was slid shut by someone out of his view.

Three days later, the door opened, and Glenda entered. They embraced each other, and Glenda said, "The baby is completely cured, Dad. It had leukemia and would have died in a week or so. Now, it's cured. The doctors won't admit that, but they do admit that there's been a complete remission."

"I'm glad of that," he said. "But what does that mean for me? And for you?" he added hastily. "And the others?"

Glenda gave him an uninterpretable look,

and said, "If you'll cooperate, Dad, we'll be set free. We can't tell the truth when we get out, and if we should slip up, we'll be in trouble. But we'll be free. If. . . ."

It was evident that she was ashamed, and yet she longed desperately for him to say yes. Nor could he blame her. She had been set free from her crooked body only to be denied the new life promised her.

"What do the others say?"

"Mom is going to go crazy, literally crazy, Dad, if she can't get out. Roger says the decision is up to you. Morna Tincrowdor says she'll do everything she can to get you out, but she's just talking, and she knows it. Leo Tincrowdor says you're not to give in to the bastards. But then he's happy. He gets all the books and booze he wants and he doesn't have to support himself. He sends a message. 'Stone walls do not a prison make.' I think he means by that you'll get out by yourself, somehow."

"If they wanted me to do something evil," he said, "I'd have to refuse, and I'm sure you wouldn't want me to say yes. But I do say yes. Only, Glenda, promise me you won't forget me. You'll write me at least once a week. And you'll come to see me once in awhile."

"Of course I will, Dad," Glenda said. "But it doesn't seem fair! You have this gift, you'll be doing good for many people, and yet you'll be kept in prison!"

"I won't be the first," he said. "Nor the last. Anyway, they're keeping me here so I won't hurt people, though God knows I don't wish anyone harm. Not consciously, anyway."

He bent close to her and whispered, "Tell Tincrowdor to keep looking. He'll know what I mean."

Late that night, he awoke knowing that someone, or something, was near and wanted him awake. He rose and went to the window and looked out over a wall and a river beyond it and a city sparkling with many lights. Near the window, perhaps twenty feet away, the saucer hung. It was whirling, and its rotation seemed to be making the noise he had heard in his sleep. The humming was modulated, and its message, so it seemed to him, was one of farewell. Farewell and sadness. It had come to earth for some unknown reason, had met with an accident, had caused an unplanned change in another creature, and now must leave. Whatever it had planted in him, it felt that the planting had not and would not come to fruition.

Suddenly, it shot upward. He thrust his face against the bars and looked up but could no longer see it. When he walked away from the window, the vision of the red fields and the green city flashed before him. Was that a vision of the thing's home? Was the vision broadcast to him by some mental means from the thing? Or, did he carry inside himself one of its progeny, and did this child carry inside itself an ancestral memory of the home of its mother? And was it able to transmit this hereditary vision to him now and then, when he, or it, or both, were under some stress?

He would never know now, he told himself. The visitor had come because of mysterious reasons and had left for mysterious reasons. Whatever her mission was, it had been aborted.

It was his fate to be the only human being touched by the stars. And it was his fate that other human beings were afraid of the startouched. So, while the giver of the two-edged gift roamed through the spaces between the stars, he, the recipient, was shut up in one small room. Forever.

"Not forever," he muttered. "You might keep me in if I was just a human being. But I'm more than that now. And you will wish you hadn't locked me up. You'll wish you had treated me like a human being."

Part 3: THE EVOLUTION OF PAUL EYRE

CHAPTER ONE

AWARE that he was being watched, Paul Eyre rolled under the bed. Here, the TV camera could not see him. The watchers would be frantic, but they would not dare to enter his cell. They did not want to drop dead.

Nude, he lay flat on his back, staring at the bedsprings and the mattress. Above the mattress were the sheets and blankets, then the roof, then the clouds. And above the clouds was the night sky. And in the sky was a star that held a planet which was his home. No, not really his home. It was the birthplace of the thing hiding in his brain, the thing causing him to change.

That thought was not quite correct. The

thing was becoming him and he was becoming the thing. The tiny yellow-brick thing in him had grown and was taking over. And he was taking it over. He and it were melding.

He was scared but not as scared as he thought he should be. Anticipation was mixed with the fright. Besides, the change was inevitable. He had seen it in dreams twelve nights in a row. The thing was communicating with him in dreams, in images and in feelings. They had no common language, but they did not need it.

His body was contracting, rounding, flattening. The flesh and the bones were softening, just as his daughter's bones had softened when he had seen her in the car in the high-school parking lot while fleeing from the police. But her skeleton had become semijelly so that she could assume, or be shaped into, human form. Not a human form, he thought, since she had been all-too-human. An acceptable human form with a straight spine and full breasts and full legs. But he was going to have a non-human form. One, in fact, which no human had ever had before.

Where would his bones and organs go?

He held up one hand under the springs. The fingernails were shimmering; the flesh was glowing. Would the watchers see the darkness under the sheets hanging over the sides dissolve before a bright light? Would they think that he had set himself on fire? And then, knowing that he had no matches or flammable fluid, would they know that he could not be on fire? They would want to send someone into his room, but they would not dare. They could only watch and wonder.

He had enough wonder for all of them. How could his one hundred and fifty pounds be altered and squeezed so without killing him? How could his brain be flattened and condensed without killing him?

His body sagged and spread out. He tried to lift his head but could not. His eyes were separating, one drifting to the left, one to the right. At the same time, his vision was becoming weaker. Only the bright light enabled him to see at all. They felt smaller, and they were starting to sink within his skull. But they could not go far because his skull was spread out and at the same time shrinking.

For a while, his eyes were at the bottoms of wells or seemed to be. He remembered reading that a man could stand at the bottom of a deep well in the daytime and see, faintly, the stars. And here came the stars. And comets. And novas. But they were within him; the nerves were flashing signals. And soon, the nerves would be gone. Or changed into a structure which the

neurologists of Earth could not understand. And changed in function, too, a function beyond their understanding.

His body moved across the floor as if it were an amoeba. Though he could not see himself, he knew that he must look as if he were becoming an amoeba. His trunk was flattening and becoming circular. His legs, his arms, his head were changing into flat, circular forms and also shrinking. He was an amoeba withdrawing its pseudopods.

Where would his brain go? What would happen to his eyes? What about his veins and arteries and capillaries? What would his bones become? His fingers? His toes? His ears? His nose? His teeth? What would become of him, Paul Eyre?

He had always believed that he had a soul. When his body died, he would ascend to heaven. Unchangeable, incorruptible, eternal Paul Eyre.

But his soul would be squeezed and flattened along with his body. Souls follow the map of the body. What the body writes, the soul reads.

And he did not know the language in which the writing was set.

He could not scream when the terror of full realization struck. He had no throat, and his lips were melted into each other.

Something within did scream then. Its voice echoed back and forth as if it were a man lost and screaming in a labyrinth deep underground. Somewhere in the dimness a form rose up and moved toward him. It was blacker than the blackness and only half-human in shape. It was menacing, yet when it spoke its voice was soft and reassuring. Paul Eyre did not want to be reassured and he wanted to run.

He felt his body swelling. A feeling of triumph and of disappointment filled him, and suddenly, he had a throat and a mouth. Instead of screaming, he whimpered.

CHAPTER TWO

At ten in the morning he awoke. He was in his pajamas and lying flat on his back on the bed. He felt tired and hungry and also ashamed. Why should he be ashamed? Was it because he was a coward?

He got out of bed and wobbled to the only door to his room. A third of the way down on this door was a smaller door. He swung this open, and a shelf holding a tray of food and milk swiveled inward. He took the tray off and shut the little door. He carried the tray to a small folding table, set it on the table and sat down in the chair before the table. While he ate ham and eggs, toast and butter, and a grapefruit, he wondered what he would have eaten if he had allowed his new form to take over. What could a being with no mouth and no digestive organs, as far as he knew, use for food? Or fuel?

There was only way to find out, a way he did not want to take. Or did he?

What he should be wondering about, he reminded himself, was why he accepted the change as reality. Once, he would have said that it was impossible. Anyone who actually thought he could change shape had to be crazy. Now, the universe seemed as flexible to him as his body.

He put the tray back on the swinging door and went into the bathroom. When he left it, he went to the doorless closet and changed from his pajamas into his clothes. At one time, he had gone into the bathroom to dress because there he would not be watched. At least, he had hoped he wasn't. Now he did not care, even if women were watching him. And that meant that he was changing not only in body but in his attitudes. Before he had been brought here, he would not have undressed before any female. Even when going to bed with his wife, he had shed his clothes in the dark so she could not see him naked.

That reminded him of some of his dreams. Though fifty-four years old, no, fifty-five now, he had a strong sex drive. He had insisted that Mavice relieve him at least three times a week. It had not mattered to him whether or not she were sick or just disinclined. It was her duty to take care of him. Mavice had usually submitted but she had complained or else been silent and had let him know through her sullenness that she was angry.

If he were to be released, he would not go back to Mavice. She hated him, though he had to admit that she had cause. But he hated her, too. Perhaps part of his hate for her was hate reflected, hate for himself. Or contempt. But there was no use thinking about that. That was in a past that seemed even more bizarre than the present.

What a pair of wretches they had been!

"Falcons in a net," Tincrowdor had once said of them. The writer was probably quoting some poem or book; his talk was half-quotation, as if he had no power to make up his own phrases. But that wasn't true. Tincrowdor had then said, "No, not falcons. You and Mavice are more like vultures in a net. Or hyenas. Or rats in a hole plugged up with cyanide."

He had hated Tincrowdor, too. No wonder that the man was afraid to meet him face to face now. Not that he blamed him. Why should Tincrowdor take a chance on dropping dead?

The sex drive had not been shut off when the door of his cell closed on him. He would have gone insane with desire if it had not been for those dreams. He would sleep, and he would see that glittering green city at the far end of many fields covered with red flowers. He would be walking across it on four feet, paws, rather. He was a creature half-human and half-feline. A leocentaur. And he was female. He had a beautiful human face, white shoulders and arms, and magnificent breasts. From the human torso down, his body was that of a lioness. A strange and powerful odor emanated from him, or rather, her. His sexual organ twitched and stank with desire. He—she—was mad with desire, but, being sentient, could control somewhat his—her —lust.

And then a great male leocentaur would come leaping and bounding across the red fields, and he—she—and the male would couple.

What a difference eight hundred pounds of feline muscle, sweating, fur, a tail, and four paws with two hands and no inhibitions made!

Eyre quivered with memory of the ecstasy, far beyond anything he had experienced as a human. He also felt shame, but, as the day passed, the shame dwindled.

He could not understand why, if he was the female, he woke up with his pajamas sticky. But the orgasms of himself, the female, in the dream were paralleled by himself, the male, in his human body. Or form.

There were other dreams, dreams in which he was a small body with a hard shell, flying through the air, flying also through emptiness where stars were the only light. He saw the stars, or, rather, felt them in a way that he could not comprehend. This "seeing" was better than "seeing" with eyes.

Did the little yellow brick in his brain carry inside it ancestral memories? Memories that it could transmit to him via dreams?

He did not know. There were many things he could not explain. For instance, the thing in him could kill or cure human beings. If it saw a diseased or crippled human being, it cured that being. If it thought it was threatened, it killed. Paul Eyre was the agent through which the thing worked, but he had no control over it.

Yet, when he had been out hunting and had fired his shotgun at the saucerthing, why hadn't it killed him? When he had searched for it afterward in those woods, why hadn't it killed him then? It could not have been in doubt about his intentions.

He thought he had wounded it. How else explain the yellow haze that issued from some opening in its side? An opening his shotgun pellets must have made.

Or had it? Tincrowdor had said that perhaps it was spawning or sporing. The cloud had been composed of microscopic quicksilver-like objects, and these were the saucerthing's young. Some had undoubtedly gone into Paul Eyre, through his nose and perhaps through his skin. They had become millions of yellow-brick-shaped things in his blood cells and in his skin tissue. He had excreted all but one, which had lodged in his brain. The others, sneezed out, digested out, sweated out, had not affected any other living being. They seemed to have died.

While in the woods, he had seen the saucer, and he had also seen the female leocentaur, a creature of unsurpassed beauty. Only now did he understand that she was the saucerthing in another shape.

He could accept that because he had to. But why hadn't the thing killed him with its thoughts or whatever power it used to kill?

If he allowed himself to become a saucer-thing, then he might understand.

Tincrowdor might have a theory. Tincrowdor was a writer whose field was mainly science fiction. When Eyre had related his experiences in the woods, Tincrowdor had given some fairly plausible theories to explain what had happened. Eyre felt that Tincrowdor had, somehow, hit close to the truth.

He would ask Tincrowdor.

Two days later, the closed circuit TV screen lit up; and a broad red face appeared. For a minute, Eyre did not recognize him. Tincrowdor had a shaggy

red and white beard, and his eyes were
sunken in black. He looked as if he had
grown a beard to disguise himself from
Death.

"Hello, Paul," he said. "They flew me in,
but the cheapos made me go second-class. I
had to buy my own champagne.

"Listen," Eyre said. "The others might
think I'm crazy, but that doesn't matter. My
situation won't be changed by their
opinions."

He paused and then said, "Last night I
almost turned into a flying saucer."

CHAPTER THREE

Tincrowdor listened without interrupting. He said, "Some years ago, I would have thought you crazy, too. Now, I'm not so sure. What the hell, I *know* you're not crazy! I'll tell you why I believe what very few can believe. A few years ago an anthropological student named Carlos Castaneda wrote three books about his experiences with Yaqui Indian magic. Put quotes around the word magic, because that's a word loaded with superstition and prejudice among Westerners. To the Yaqui *brujos*, sorcerers we'd call them, there are many worlds coexistent with ours. Parallel worlds, if you will, which intersect ours. By use of their quote magic unquote, the *brujos* can use entities, or forces, in these other worlds. Castaneda called these worlds nonordinary reality. That is, they are realities which we don't usually encounter.

"I won't go into how these *brujos* can perform their so-called magic. It's not magic, but a rigid and always dangerous science. Or a discipline. Never mind the terms. The thing is that the *brujos* Castaneda knew, Don Juan and Don Genaro and some others, could peform incredible feats. They had powers we Westerners have always thought were mumbo-jumbo, fantasies, superstitions. Castaneda was convinced that the powers existed, have existed since the Old Stone Age. For instance, and I cite only one because it is relevant to your case, the *brujos* can change themselves into birds and fly. I became convinced after reading his books that they can do this. Castaneda is a level-headed scientist and no hoaxer."

"You mean that I met a creature from this, this nonordinary reality, and that it has made these changes in me?" Eyre said.

Tincrowdor shook his head. "Not entirely. You have met a nonordinary creature and are undergoing some nonordinary changes. But these are not of the nature which Castaneda described. Your saucerthing and your sphinx come from this world, this hard universe. They are nonordinary only because they have just arrived. Probably, many things here are nonordinary to them, or it, I should say, since the forms seem to be metamorphous, not discrete.

"Apparently, the yellow-thing in you is capable of causing these changes in shape. It may not derive its power solely from itself. We human beings may have this power but have never realized it. Rather, only a few have ever realized it. The devices exist in our bodies, and the yellow-thing knows how to use them.

"Here's what I think the situation could be. Postulate a species of sentient, or maybe nonsentient, beings which can live in space. They can also travel through space, perhaps using gravitons as a means of propulsion. Gravitons are wavicles. Wavicles are phenomena which act as if they're both frequency waves and particles. Gravitons are wavicles responsible for gravity, just as photons are wavicles responsible for light. Well, that doesn't matter. It's not how they can propel themselves through space and atmosphere but their biological setup that is important.

"I can't guess at how they have sexual intercourse and have children with genes from male and female. Maybe they have a sexual-reproductive process that isn't remotely like what we know on Earth. Anyway, these ufos, let's call them that and not flying saucers, these ufos, originated on some planet or maybe in space. Their planet was long ago crowded, or else they have a drive to seed other planets. In any event, many leave their native world. They go to other planets that are like Earth. These have sentients. Some are humanoids. Some centauroids. Some are only God knows what.

"The pregnant female lands and releases the eggbearing cloud. The microscopic eggs, or spore, or what have you, enter the tissues of sentients. Only one of the millions of eggs in a sentient's body survives, just as only one sperm out of millions in an ejaculation survives to unite with an ovum in the womb. Whoever gets to the brain first is the winner.

"The egg and the sperm, that's you, Paul, a bidpedal thinking sperm, unite. The process is half-fusion, half-symbiosis. You think it's parasitism because you're an unwilling and very conscious host. A reluctant spermatozoan. Strange things happen. You have the power to cure or kill even when unconscious or sleeping. Only it's not being done by you but by the ufo-egg, which goes all the way in its healing or its self-defense.

"Why does the symbiote kill those who threaten you? Obviously because it's protecting itself and you, the host. Why does it heal nonthreatening humans? Obviously because it regards them as future hosts, or sperm.

"And so you're shut up in a prison hospital for observation by scientists who can't belive what they're seeing but have to believe.

"Meanwhile, the zygote becomes embryo becomes an adult. The adult is, or will be, the ufo-egg plus the host. My analogies are, biologically speaking, mixed up. A symbiote, or parasite, and its hosts are not two gametes. But this doesn't matter. You get the idea. You start to change shape. You resist, but you will eventually go all the way. You will become a saucerthing. What will happen to the brain in that saucer? I don't know. I suspect you'll become half-human, half-alien. You'll grow to like your powers. After all, it's only human to desire powers that other humans don't have. Nor will you be bound to one shape. At times, maybe whenever you wish, you can change back to your original shape.

"That the saucer you saw changes into the shape of its original leocentaur form demonstrates that.

"Then, one day, you get out of this prison. You either stay on Earth to look for a male or go out into space for a male. You get fertilized, how, don't ask me. You spread your seed. Other humans suffer the same strange space-change that you have suffered. And so on. Eventually, we have an

Earth populated by ufo-humans. What happens then? I don't know. I suspect that some will take off into space to seek virgin planets."

Eyre said, "You don't believe that."

Tincrowdor said, "Do you believe it?"

"I don't know," Eyre said. "I do know that I don't like it."

CHAPTER FOUR

That was not the end of the conversation. What about the ufos? Why had so many been sighted and why, if there were so many, hadn't any man been affected by them, as Eyre now was?

"I don't know that any have actually been sighted here," Tincrowdor said. "The Air Force investigation explained away all but about two percent as misinterpreted natural phenomena, delusions, hoaxes, or the result of mass hysteria. That an unexplainable two percent remains might be due to the investigators' failure of rationalizing powers. Or perhaps the two percent were composed of actual ufos. These could have been males looking for females, which weren't at that time on Earth."

"But they weren't all of the same type," Eyre said. "Some were balls that acted more like electrical phenomena than anything. Some where cigar-shaped. Some had blinking lights. Almost all were much larger than the saucer I saw."

Tincrowdor shrugged and said, "If they existed in some place other than the observer's mind, they may have belonged to different species or genera than your saucer. Or perhaps the males have different shapes. Maybe the differing types were hostile toward each other. They may have exterminated each other in a secret unseen war or perhaps declared Earth a dangerous area and so avoid it from now on. Maybe they have a treaty that has declared Earth off-limits, and your saucer was here illegally. Or maybe she was sick or out of food and had to land here.

"You want me to explain all about them, and I can't even tell you all about the how and why of human beings. Besides, everything I've said may be wrong."

Tincrowdor seemed to find this amusing. Eyre did not.

When the dialogue was ended, Eyre paced back and forth—he could not sit still long unless he was reading or watching TV—and wondered what the effect of the conversation would be on the authorities. Would they assume he was crazy? If they did, then they would do nothing. Things would proceed as they had been. They might want to give him therapy, but they would be afraid to try. If they believed his story, then they might become so alarmed that they would try to kill him. They would justify murder as in the best interest of the majority. The majority: all humanity with the exception of Paul Eyre. Logically, he had to agree with them.

CHAPTER FIVE

The following morning, Tincrowdor's face appeared again on the screen. He looked pale and frightened.

"Paul," he said, "you've been told that, if it looks as if you might escape, cyanide gas will be released in your room. It's a terrible thing, but *they* can't allow you even to get out into the hall. They're afraid they couldn't stop you, since you can kill with a glance. Well, last night. . . ."

He paused and swallowed, then said, "Last night one of *them* made up his own mind to take action. Apparently, he believed what we said yesterday. He sneaked into the room in which the valves and the off-on button controlling the

cyanide gas are located. This is guarded by
one man, and an alarm is set off if any
unathorized person enters. He bludgeoned
the guard and made a dash for the controls.
He had to turn two valves before he could
press the release button. He never got the
first valve turned. As he touched it, he
dropped dead. Now tell me. Did you somehow know all this was going on?"

Eyre was silent for a moment, then he
said, "Not at all."

Tincrowdor swallowed again and said,
"Well, you see the implications, don't you?"

Eyre could not keep the exultation out of
his voice.

"Yes, I—this thing in me, rather—can kill
even if I can't see the one who's threatening
me."

A few seconds later, the shock hit him. He
sat down trembling. People were actually
trying to kill him. Yet he had done nothing
except to defend himself. No, he had not
done even that. It was the creature inside
him. But even as he thought that, he knew
that that was not true. There was no longer
any clearly defined Paul Eyre or ufo-child.
Their borders were dissolving; their
identities were merging.

He had to get out and away, but to do that
he had to experience something the thought
of which terrified him.

"They," Tincrowdor said, "are divided.
Half think you are telling the truth; half

think you're crazy. But the latter half isn't certain. They saw the bright light emanating from under the bed, and they do know that it wasn't caused by fire. Your room is monitored for any change in temperature, and there was none then. That was a cold light."

"Why aren't Polar and Kowalski talking to me?" Eyre said. "Why have you suddenly become the spokesman?"

"I don't have a degree in science, but I do have a free-wheeling imagination. This is a situation which requires a mind that is at ease with the fantastic. Set a thief to catch a thief. Put a science-fiction author in a science-fiction situation. Besides, I don't think they trust me to keep my mouth shut. They can watch me while I'm working for them."

"Are you actually going to help them to kill me?" Eyre said.

Tincrowdor looked distressed.

"I don't think you can be killed."

"But you're willing to try," Eyre said.

Tincrowdor was silent.

Eyre said, "And you're the one who was always raising hell because the U.S. was needlessly killing so many in Vietnam. You're the one who was too tender-hearted to shoot deer."

Tincrowdor was obviously frightened. For all he knew, he might drop dead at this moment. Actually, Eyre thought, Tincrowdor wasn't as cowardly and soft-hearted as he had supposed him to be. He must have courage to be able to tell him all this and to chance making him angry.

Or perhaps Tincrowdor wanted to be struck dead. He felt guilt because he had not made the public aware of what was being done to Eyre. This guilt was increased by his participation in the imprisonment of Eyre. Moreover, he could not keep from trying to figure out ways to kill the unkillable. It was a challenge to the intellect, which he had no doubt justified with all sorts of rationalization.

Suddenly Eyre realized that the face on the screen belonged to his most dangerous enemy.

That knowledge was followed by a slight shock. Why hadn't Tincrowdor fallen dead?

Could it because Tincrowdor was also secretly rooting for him? Tincrowdor had once said that it would be a good thing if something did wipe out all of mankind. Insanity, grief, sorrow, greed, murder, rape, brutality, hopelessness, despair, prejudice, hypocrisy, and persecution would vanish from Earth. Tincrowdor had admitted that poetry, art, and music would also disappear, but the price paid for a few worthwhile poems, dramas, paintings, sculptures, and symphonies wasn't worth it. Besides, very few people appreciated art. According to him, money, power, and tearing other people apart, verbally and physically, were what most people cared about.

"On the other hand," Tincrowdor had said, "if man goes, love and compassion also go. Perhaps we're just a stage in evolution toward a species all of whose members will be filled with love and compassion. But I ask our Creator why, if this is true, we stages have to suffer so? Don't we count for anything?"

Tincrowdor had once written a short story, *What You See*, in which visitors from the star Algol, as a parting gift, had spread an aerosol all over Earth. This covered all the mirrors in the world, and whenever anybody looked on one, he saw himself as he truly was. This did not have the desired effect of causing changes for the better in the viewers of self. Instead, all mirrors were smashed and a law passed making it a capital offense to manufacture mirrors. The law wasn't necessary. Nobody except a few masochists wanted mirrors.

Eyre had asked Tincrowdor why, if he felt that way, he didn't commit suicide.

"I like to make myself and others miserable," the writer had said.

And now Tincrowdor was torn in two. He wanted to survive and hence wanted Eyre to die. He also wanted Eyre to survive, because he might be the next stage in man's evolution.

That Eyre could perceive this meant that he *had* evolved in one respect. There was a time when he would have been too dull to see what was troubling Tincrowdor. Eyre was, had been, an engineer who could analyze malfunctions in machines down to the last nut and bolt. But troubleshooting people had been beyond him. They were impenetrable and irrational.

CHAPTER SIX

That night, Eyre awoke from a sleep untroubled by dreams. He rose, drank some water, and went to the single window to look at the night scene. The stars were out, the river beyond the walls and the city on both sides of the river were speckled and striped with lights. Like a zebra with the measles, he thought.

Between his building and the high stone walls was a paved area. This was bright with floodlights on the building and the wall. A tower at a corner of the walls to his left thrust up like the hand of a traffic cop signaling for a stop. It held two guards armed with rifles, and a machine gun.

He was surprised, though not shocked, to

see the female leocentaur standing on the pavement below. The light gleamed whitely on her bare upper trunk, blackly on her long hair and tawnily on the leonine under-body. She was smiling up at him and waving with one hand.

The last time he had seen her, she had been a saucershaped thing hanging in the air outside his window. From her whirling body had come a sound that had seemed to him a farewell. But he had been mistaken. She was still around, still watching over him. Like a mother over her child.

Shouts came from the watchtower. She bounded to one side as rifle bullets struck the pavement and then she loped away out of Eyre's sight to the right. A moment later, the machine gun opened up, but, after five bursts, it stopped. There were no more shots, but there was much excitement.

Three-quarters of an hour after the guards and the dogs had quit running around on the pavement, Tincrowdor's face filled the TV.

"Up to now I've been a sort of John the Baptist for a weird messiah," he said. "Faith was noticeable only by its absence. But they believe *now*! They've not only got two eye witnesses, but they've got photographs! The watchtower was equipped with a motion picture camera, you know. No, you wouldn't. Anyway here are some stills."

The first was of the leocentauress running away. The third showed her leaping high into the air. At least fifteen feet, Eyre estimated. The fifth showed an elongated blur. The next one was of a blurred but undeniably saucer-shaped object. The last showed the saucer as it shot by a floodlight.

"Apparently, she didn't think she was really in danger," Tincrowdor said. "Otherwise, the guards would be dead. Of course, it may be that the adult isn't capable of killing through ESP means or however it's done. In which case, you, if you become an adult, may no longer be a danger. At least, not one kind of danger. You'll always be a menace."

"One reason I think that the adult form may not be able to kill is that you didn't kill the guards. You, that thing is you, anyway, must have wanted to protect its mother. So why didn't it do it?

"Or is there something we don't know?"

Eyre repressed any show of joy at the mother's escape. He said, "So what happens now?"

"I don't know. I think they're going to let the White House in on what's been going on. They've been very secretive so far. Very few officials know that a man is being held without any judicial processes at all and with no consideration of his civil rights. And fewer yet know the real reason why.

But now that they have evidence that even the most unimaginative will have to accept, they will have to inform the highest authority. It may take some time to convince *him*, though."

What you're not saying, Eyre thought, is that everybody in the know is going to be scared to death. To my death.

And that morning, while it was still dark, he undressed and went under the bed. Sometime later he emerged, shaking, weak, and frightened. Halfway through, he had quit. For a long time, he lay in bed, tossing and turning, and cursing himself for a weakling. Yet he was glad that something in him, himself this time, had refused to become nonhuman. He finally fell asleep, waking at ten-thirty. He ate breakfast and read several pages of a book on a tribe in highland New Guinea. He had been reading much and widely of late, trying to make up for all the years when he had read only the daily local newspaper and sports magazines.

As he began pacing back and forth, the closed-circuit TV came on. Tincrowdor said, "This'll be the last time I'll be seeing you, Paul. Here, anyway. I'm quitting. I don't want anything more to do with these people. Or with you. I can't take it any longer. I'm being ripped apart between my conscience and what I believe, logically, should be done with you. And this last incident is too much for me. It was my idea, I'll admit, but I didn't like it when it was put in practice."

"What last idea?" Paul said.

Somebody out of sight said something to Tincrowdor. He snarled, "What the hell's the difference?" and turned back to Eyre. "I suggested a device to turn on the cyanide by a remote control machine. And they installed one. Two, rather. The light-sensing monitor on you was to send a radio signal to a machine in Washington, D.C., when it detected that glow from under the bed. This in turn would signal back to the automatic controller of the cyanide-release machine. The setup was arranged so that there would be no human agency involved in the actual operation of gas release. That way, no one would die, they hoped."

He swallowed, looked contrite, and said, "I did it, Paul, because I'm human! I want humanity to survive! As humans. Better the devil you know, I thought. And anyway, I didn't believe that you could be killed, and I wanted to find out if I was wrong. I hoped I was at the same time I hoped I wasn't. Can you understand?"

"I suppose that if I were in your shoes, I'd do the same." Eyre said. "But you can't expect me to be very friendly with a man who's been trying to kill me."

"Of course I don't. I'm not very friendly to myself just now. But here's what happened. As soon as the lights glowed, a signal was sent to the machine in Washington. That machine never got to send a signal back. Both it and the control device here burned up! The circuits apparently became overloaded and burst into flames. They had fused but it made no difference. Up they went!"

"You can keep on trying, and you'll never succeed," Eyre said.

He was startled. He had had no intention of saying that. Was the thing in him talking? Or was the merger, the fusion as Tincrowdor called it, almost complete?

"Listen, Paul!" Tincrowdor shouted. "That window is shatterproof, but you can get through it! Their plan. . . ."

A hand clamped down on Tincrowdor's mouth. Polar and Kowalski appeared behind him and dragged him, struggling, out of sight.

Eyre wished Polar and Kowalski dead, but a moment later Polar appeared. Eyre was glad that he had not killed him. Perhaps it was better that he had no control over his powers. The responsibility and the guilt were not his.

"I assure you, Eyre, that we're not planning anything more," Polar said in a high-pitched voice. "Not against you, not in a positive manner, I mean. We know we can't do anything to you. So we're just going to keep you here until, by the grace of

God, we can reach a satisfactory solution."

Polar was lying, of course.

"Die! Die!" Eyre shouted, forgetting in another burst of anger his gladness of a moment ago.

Polar screamed and ran out of sight. A moment later, the screen went blank. Eyre quit laughing and stretched out on the floor. He closed his eyes but opened them almost at once. This time, the light was coming not from his skin but from deep within himself. And it was not steady but pulsing.

There was horror again, though it was as much less as the light was more. Or so it seemed to him. And the metamorphosis went so swiftly that his head would have swum—if he had had a head. Suddenly, he didn't. It had collapsed and withdrawn and changed.

He rose from the floor humming. He was rotating or at least aware that he was, but he had at the same time no sense of dizziness or disorientation. Without eyes, he could see. The room around him was a black sphere, not a cube. The furniture was violet bowls. The electrical wiring within the walls was helixes of pulsing blue. The window was hexagonal, and the light from the flood lights was mauve, and the stars were of many colors and many shapes. One was a huge russet doughnut.

He had no hands to feel his shell, but he

could feel with a sense strange to him. The shell was far more resistant than steel but as flexible as rubber.

He thought, "Forward," and the shatter-proof glass flew out in front of him, the shards flaming and falling like comets with green tails. As they struck the yellow pavement below, they became brown.

If he had had a voice, he would have shouted with exultation. Instead, a tiny electric spark seemed to pass through him. It glowed as it traveled from one edge of his shell to the other, sputtered, and was gone.

Where were his eyes, his ears, his arms, his legs, his mouth, his genitals? Who cared? He certainly did not, as he swept out and up, curving almost vertically into the air. His change of angle brought visions of a lightning streak, colored scarlet. He was riding on it. Below, machine-gun bullets made orange pyramids that became increasingly brown as gravity carried them back to Earth. When they landed, they became flat hexagons.

Babies play, and Eyre played for a long time. Up and down, in and out, skimming the fields, climbing above the atmosphere where the sun blazed azure and space blazed greenly, down again, the air moving around him like snow on a TV screen, the snow melting as he slowed down, down into a river, moving through the blood-colored water, fishes pentagons of dark violet, the weeds upside-down beige towers of Babel. And up and out again, through clouds that looked like cerulean toadstools.

He did not get tired or hungry. Exerting or resting, he was "feeding." He did not understand how he did it, any more than a savage would understand the processes by which food entering his mouth became energy and flesh. All he knew was that, munching mouthlessly, he devoured photons and gravitons and chronotrons and radio waves and magnetic lines of force. When in space, he would be eating all these and x-ray energy. His mouth was his shell.

As an engineer, he would have supposed that the surface area of his shell was too small to absorb enough energy to keep him alive. As what he now was, he knew that he could take in more than enough energy.

And then, as he soared up in a catenary curve that left behind a mile-long line of glimmering sapphire porcupine quills, quickly fading, he saw his mother. Going three times as fast, she was an ankh-shaped thing, striped with scarlet and blue and trailing yellow energy particles shaped like stars of David. She did not slow down, she went on up, she whispered—or so it seemed to him—that he should follow her. She would love to have him accompany her. If he did not wish to, however, she bade him a fond farewell and hello.

"And what shall we do, brother?" he said

in his nonvoice.

His brother did not answer. The little yellow thing in him was he; his brother was he, and he was his brother.

He turned and raced around the planet, which was a shifting pattern of triangles and cubes below him. He sped in his orbit as if circularity was a means for arriving at a decision.

And it was.

CHAPTER SEVEN

The doorbell rang.

Mavice Eyre got up from her chair before the TV set and walked through babble and smoke to the front door. She opened it onto the night and Paul Eyre. Two seconds passed, during which he could have covered fifty miles while out of the atmosphere and in the other form. Then Mavice fainted.

There was confusion and consternation. Paul Eyre acted calmly and did what had to be done. With order restored, the TV set off, and Mavice and his children, Roger and Glenda, in their chairs, he began to tell them a little of what had happened. Of his metamorphosis, he said nothing.

When he had finished, Mavice said, "Why

didn't *they* tell us that they were letting you go? Why didn't *you* phone us? I almost died when I saw you!"

"They would like to keep this a secret," he said. "Your oaths of silence still hold. I'm well now, though I'm not what I was. Not by a long shot. And I didn't notify you I was coming because they asked me not to. Why, I don't know. Security reasons, I suppose."

He could not tell them the truth, of course.

There was a silence. His wife and his son were still afraid of him. Glenda did not fear him, but she did not trust him all the way. Of the three, she suspected that he was far more changed than he had admitted.

"Dad, where'd you get those clothes?" Roger said. "They look as if they came off a skid-row bum. And they sure smell like it!"

"I'll get rid of them," he said. And he thought, they did come from a wino. I took his clothes and in return I cured his diseased liver and his incipient tuberculosis and I may have altered the chemical imbalance that has made him an alcoholic. Maybe. I don't know what was sick about him. But if he had a cirrhosed liver and that cough was from TB and his lust for drink comes from chemistry and not from the psyche, then he's healed.

"Are you going back to work at Trackless Diesel, Dad?" Glenda said.

"Never. The idea makes me sick."

"But what will you do?" Mavice said shrilly. "You're fifty-five, and in only ten years you'll be able to retire! If you quit, you'll lose your retirement pension and the group medical insurance and. . . ."

"I have better things to do," he said.

"Such as what?" Mavice said.

"Such as finding out what a human being is and why he is," Eyre said. "Before I go on."

"Go on where?" Glenda asked.

"Wherever my destiny takes me."

"And what is that?"

"Whatever seems to be best. Or whatever is good."

"Look, Dad," Glenda said. She stood up. "Look at me. I was a cripple and a hunchback, and you healed me just by looking at me! Think of what you can do for others!"

Glenda was radiant with joy, but Roger and Mavice had a better foundation for their emotion than Glenda did for hers. Not that they should be so afraid of him. They should dread what others would try to do to him and then to them. Perhaps he should not have come back here. He had put them in jeopardy, whereas, if he had gone to some distant place, they would be safe.

But that wasn't true either. As long as he stayed on Earth, no human was safe. Change was dangerous, and he was here to

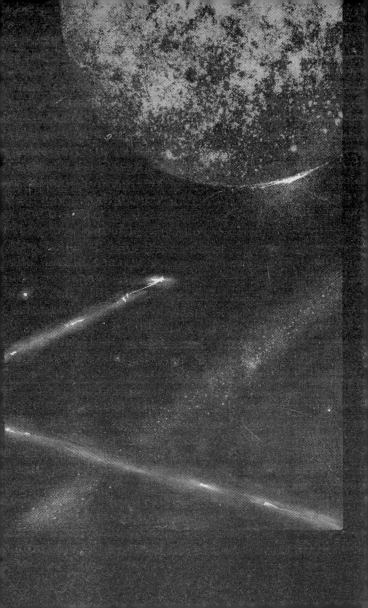

see that all were changed. It didn't matter if he went to Timbuktu (and he might), change would spread out from him in an all-engulfing wave. It would lap over the Earth.

He stood up. "Let's go to bed. Tomorrow. . . ."

Mavice said, "Yes . . .?"

"I begin looking."

Mavice assumed that he meant he would search for another job. It was his duty to support his family.

And so it was. But a far stronger duty was to find a mate. And then the seeding would begin.

Part Four:
PASSING ON

CHAPTER ONE

WINDLIKE, ghostlike, he raced around the earth.

When he was human, Earth was solid and horizon-bound. When he was saucer, it was a complex pattern of shifting triangle and cubes. Land was dully glowing chestnut and silver. Water was brightly glowing scarlet and gold. The three-cornered shapes and hollow cubes of land were smaller than those of water. The Gulf Stream was the same color as the rest of the Atlantic, but the cubes orbited more closely around the triangles.

Clouds of water were toadstools. Smog was a herd of shapes like porcupine fish. The clear air, of which there was very little,

was like the snow on the screen of a mal-
functioning TV set. Rain and snow alike
were polyhedrons, but rain was azure and
snow was burnt orange.

That was as "seen" from the strato-
sphere. When he raced close to the earth,
the triangles and cubes merged, became
still, became shades of green. The trees
were upside-down pyramids, looking more
like strangely shaped tumors of the earth
than separate entities.

At times he slowed down and eased up to
a house. He "looked" into the windows.
Dogs resembled astrakhans; cats, gas jets;
humans, the symbols on the dollar bill,
pyramids with one great crimson eye,
always expanding or shrinking.

Around and around, up and down. And
nowhere another of his kind. He should
have accepted the invitation of his
"mother," and thus he could have
journeyed through space to the planet of
some far-off star with her as a companion
and guide. Now, if he lived a thousand
years, and he would, he might never see
another of his own. On the other hand (only
a figure of speech, since he had no hands in
this form), he might run into a dozen the
day after tomorrow. The night after
tomorrow, rather, since he flew only late at
night. In the daytime of the United States of
America, he walked on two legs.

He did not need sleep. To metamorphose

was to lose the need for sleep. Something
happened in his altered body which did
away with the toxins accumulated as biped.
the ones whose convalescence would take
anything about this. And "the Eyrecraft
with the sapphire quills that traced the
change of angle in his flight.

A falling star, he shot toward his apartment, braked with a flare of white-edged
blue comets, stopped before the open
window, and entered. The transition was so
quick that any human eye would have seen
only a blur. And he was in the form which
billions knew as Paul Eyre.

CHAPTER TWO

Being human had its advantages. When he sped like a saucer-shaped Santa Claus from pole to pole, he browsed on photons, gravitons, X rays, magnetic lines, and chronotrons. But they were tasteless. Not so the buttered toast, the crisp bacon, the fried egg, the cantaloupe, the coffee. Intake was delicious, and so was output. Before the change, he had excreted with haste and shame, though he had been too dull to know that was the situation. Now he experienced a new ecstasy; getting rid of was not the same as taking in, but it was just as pleasurable. He shaved, showered, and dressed, read for four hours and, at seven-thirty, walked out of his apartment. The day manager and the guards said hello and looked at him with a barely concealed dislike, fear, and awe. Ostensibly, they were there to protect him. Actually, they were protecting the others from him. The others were the rest of humanity.

Practically, they were incapable of protecting him or the others.

He walked out of the building. Across the street was another apartment building. It held rooms in which many dozens of people, around the clock, trained cameras or listened to wire taps or swiveled directional microphones. He had "seen" them at night, their pulsing eyes glowing. They were reporting to various agencies in Washington, in Europe, and in Asia. They spied on him and on each other.

He walked swiftly twelve blocks and turned into a driveway leading to a huge old mansion. Once it had belonged to a rich family, then it had been a funeral home, and now it was his headquarters. The crowd along the driveway and on the porch cheered as he walked among them. They reached out their hands, though they never touched him. He made a gesture that they should draw back, and they surged like a wave withdrawing from a beach. They loved him, and they hated him.

Of the thousands or so on the parking lot, the grounds, the sidewalk, and the porch, half were the lame, the halt, the blind, the dying. The others were relatives or friends or the hired, bringing those on crutches, stretchers, and wheelchairs. He could, and would, send most of the sick home with their diseases left behind as abandoned baggage. But what could he do for the others, those defined as healthy? What could he do for greed, hate, prejudice, and self-loathing?

Lepers all.

He stopped on the porch, turned around, and held up his hand. Silence floated. "Go home now!" he said. "Make way for the others!"

There were cries of joy and amazement. Crutches soared. Men and women danced and cried. Children stood up from wheelchairs. Some, still on stretchers, were rushed to waiting ambulances. They were the ones whose convalescence would take some time. A woman whose misshapen bones were beginning to jell cried out in fear. But she would be all right in a few weeks.

A man near the foot of the steps to the porch suddenly reached into his coat pocket and brought out a revolver. His face was pale and contorted.

"Die, you filthy anti-Christ!" he screamed. "Die and go to hell!"

Hate was snatched away by pain. He dropped the revolver and clutched at his chest. Two plainsclothesmen moved toward him, but they were too late. He was dead on the sidewalk by the time they had reached him.

Paul Eyre murmured, "They never learn!"

CHAPTER THREE

In the beginning, he had sat in a large office while the "patients" walked by or were carried before him. They had entered one door and without pausing or speaking proceeded to the exit. There was no business to transact except that of getting people in and out as swiftly as possible. Each was handed a card which stated that if the recipient cared to, he could send whatever sum he felt like sending to this address. Paul Eyre did not doubt that among his employees were agents of the American Medical Association and the Food and Drug Administration. They watched him as if he were a hawk among chickens and he owner of the chickens. But their reports were monotonous, unspiced by irregularities.

After a few months, Eyre had moved out onto the porch. In warm weather, he looked at the passersby through screens. In cold weather, the porch was glassed in. Automobiles, trucks, and buses crept by on the horse-shaped driveway and the street while he looked at the pale and hopeful faces in them. To heal, he had to see them in the flesh, though a single glance sufficed.

On the other hand, he did not have to see to kill. Snipers hidden in rooms many stories above him fell dead as they put their finger on the trigger. An automatic device set to gas him, operating by a time clock so there would be no direct human initiation, had gone up in smoke. A suicidal fanatic had tried to fly his nitroglycerine-loaded airplane into his headquarters, but it had blown up while over the Illinois River. A time bomb had exploded in the face of a man before he could get it into his car.

There had doubtless been many other fatal incidents about which Paul Eyre knew nothing.

That was, to him, the strange thing about his powers. He had not the slightest idea how they operated. There was no tickling, no tingling, no change in body temperature, no outward or inward manifestation of energy transmitted or withdrawn.

He had established, however, that he did not kill just because he disliked or hated a person. The power was activated only when a person was about to be an immediate physical danger to him.

He was an enigma for more than himself. Everybody, even the Indian in the remote Amazon jungle or the aborigine in the great Australian desert, had heard of him. They came from everywhere, and business in Busiris, Illinois, boomed. Every motel, hotel, and rooming house was jammed. Motels and restaurants were going up like telephone poles. The police department had had to double its traffic division, but there were no outcries from the taxpayers. Eyre was paying for the new personnel. There were protests from Eyre's neighbors about the crowded streets, but nobody could do anything about this. And "the Eyrecraft industry," as the local paper termed it, had brought prosperity to Busiris. It was the largest industry in the county, larger even than the giant Trackless Diesel Motor Corporation for which Eyre had once worked.

And so he sat on the porch, even during his lunch period, or paced back and forth while the sick were carried by. At seven in the evening, he walked off the porch. His staff would stay for another two or three hours to complete their work. But he was through for the day; ten hours and thirty-odd thousand people were enough for him. Too much. He was exhausted though he had done nothing except sit, walk, and confer with his manager and secretaries occasionally. He walked home without a bodyguard, though the sidewalks and streets would be crowded with the sick, waiting for him to see them.

He dined alone in his apartment except for the three evenings a week that his current mistresses visited him. These were beautiful young women who had their peculiar reasons for wanting to bed with him. Some were grateful because he had healed them or relatives or husbands. Some felt they adored him because he was a miracle worker. Some, he found out later, were agents for the AMA, the IRS, the FBI, Russia, China, Cuba, England, Israel, the United Arab Republic, Germany (West and East), and India. Some had even asked him to take refuge in their countries. Their countries had tried to kidnap him, with fatal results for the agent, so now they were trying to seduce him. He never turned them over to the FBI (in one case, the young woman was working for both Albania and the FBI). He merely told them to leave and quit bothering him.

Sometimes, he would go to the window and look down at the street. It was white with faces turned up to him as if he were the sun and they the plants. Their murmur came up to him even through the soundproofing. "Heal me," it cried, "and I will be happy."

He knew better, but he healed them anyway. He couldn't help himself.

Somebody had once suggested that he fly over the world while the sick were brought out into the open spaces for him to look down upon. He had rejected this. Even if he could cover every square foot of the planet in a single day, he would have a million new patients the next day. But to travel by plane around and around the globe would be to lose all his privacy. How could he leave his quarters at night and girdle the earth, search the skies, sublunary space, Africa, Polynesia, and the South Pole? No, here at least, he had made arrangements to leave by the back window which faced a court where no one could come. No doubt, it was under electronic and photographic surveillance. But his watchers were government officials, and their reports were top secret. They didn't believe what they reported. Some things are so impossible that to admit you believe them is to admit that you're crazy. Between the two was a credibility fuse easily blown in human beings.

Why had Paul Eyre become the great healer? Why had he subjected himself to a boring duty which could never achieve its goal, the extermination of all physical diseases in mankind? For one thing, he didn't have the heart to turn the sick away. For another, he was getting rich, and he needed much money to pay for the support of his daughter and his ex-wife. And, last, but by no means least, he was, being human when in human form, gratified by the attention and the idolization. He was the most important man on the planet. Important in a way which the public did not even suspect. If they had, they would have tried to tear him apart, literally. He shuddered when he thought of it, not because the mob would succeed, because they wouldn't. It was the vision of hundreds, perhaps thousands, dropping dead at the same time that sickened him. So far, the few known deaths, his would-be murderers, had been explained away as caused by excitement combined with a weak heart. Though none of his attackers had had heart trouble, fake medical histories had been supplied. The pathologists who did the dissections did not have to be bribed to validate these. They always found the heart ruptured, even when it looked healthy.

Eyre read for a while after eating the meal ordered from a delicatessen. (No need to test it; the poisoner would have died before he could touch the food.) He put the book aside and watched TV for half an hour, then turned it off. How trivial even his favorite programs seemed. Bullshit and nonsense, as his friend, Tincrowdor, was fond of saying.

Tincrowdor. Was he a friend? When Eyre had been held in prison, Tincrowdor had helped him. At the same time, Tincrowdor had thought of ways to kill him. But that, Tincrowdor had explained, had been done because he did not really believe that Eyre could be killed. Besides, the intellectual challenge had been too much for him. He had to try.

He went to the phone and called the switchboard downstairs. He waited, while the ringing went on and on. How many were listening in? At least a dozen American government agencies, the AMA, and half a dozen foreign agents. Trolls eavesdropping on the troll killer. Helpless to do anything but listen and then make their reports.

At last, a boozy male voice answered. "Leo Queequeg Tincrowdor, poet laureate of B-T-A-O-C, speaking."

If the unwary caller asked what the letters meant, Tincrowdor would reply, "Busiris, the asshole of creation."

"Come on over," Eyre said. "I'd like to talk to you."

"You're not mad at me?"

"I just want to talk. That is, if you're fairly sober."

"I'm fairly," Tincrowdor said. "Tell your

gorillas not to shoot."

"They're just here to watch me," Eyre said, "not to protect me. You could come in with a bazooka, and they'd only ask you to produce your ID." Which was not much of an exaggeration.

CHAPTER FOUR

Before Tincrowdor arrived, another visitor phoned from the lobby. This was Dr. Lehnhausen, the righthand man of the President of the United States. Eyre was surprised, thought not very much. Lehnhausen had made unannounced trips before, flying in secretly from Washington, talking to him for an hour or so, and then departing as swiftly as he had come.

A minute later, Eyre admitted Lehnhausen. Four men stood guard, two by the door, one at the elevator, and one at the end of the hall, near the fire escape.

Lehnhausen was a tall, dark man with a slight German accent. He waved his hand at Eyre and said, "How are you, sir?"

"I'm never sick, and I'm always busy," Eyre said. "And you?"

"That depends upon what you tell me," Lehnhausen said. "I'm here to ask you to reconsider your decision. *He* told me that he hoped you would remember that you are an American."

How I would have thrilled at those words only a year ago! Eyre thought. The President himself asking me to do my duty, to defend my country.

"I never said no," Eyre said. "I thought I'd made that clear. What I did say, and you were there and know it, is that it's not necessary for me to live in Washington or to be advised by a bunch of generals and bureaucrats. I will defend this nation, but it will be done automatically. And it doesn't matter where I am."

"Yes, we understand that," Lehnhausen said. "But what if the President believes that it is necessary to launch an atomic missile attack before another nation does?"

"I don't know," Eyre said. He began to pace back and forth and to sweat. "I have tried repeatedly to explain that I have no control over this, this power. Anything that is an immediate threat to me seems to be killed. An atomic war would threaten me, even if the attack were launched from this country at another one. The enemy would retaliate, of course, and that would be a threat. To stop this, I, or whatever is working inside me, might decide that the man who gives the word to attack should drop dead before he can give that word.

"This means that whoever starts to give the word, to press the button, would die. Which means that there is no need for the President to order an attack. The attack he would be trying to forestall would never come. The enemy executive would die before he could give the order. The man succeeding him would die, and so on.

"So there is no call for the President to give his order. Do you see what I mean? God knows I've told you enough times, and I find this visit unnecessary and annoying. I can't seem to get the truth through to you people in Washington."

Lehnhausen said, bitterly, "What you have done is to nullify our atomic potential. We can't use it, and that places us at a disadvantage with nations which have a greater potential in conventional means of warfare. Both the Soviet Union and China can assemble far larger armies than we can. The Soviet Union's navy is larger than ours. Russia could take over Europe at any time, and there is nothing we could do about it. And China could take over Asia. Then what would happen?"

"I don't know," Eyre said. "Perhaps I—this thing in me, rather—might decide that an invasion of the Old World by these two powers would be an immediate threat to me. It might kill the Chinese or Russian leaders before they could give the order to attack. I don't know. I do know that it would probably decide that an invasion of this country by any power would be an immediate threat. In which case, there wouldn't be any invasion."

"But there might be one of the Old World, and you'd do nothing," Lehnhausen said.

"You make me sound like a traitor," Eyre said. "Can't I convince you that I have absolutely no control? Anyway, you have told me that the foreign governments have found out all this, and they won't attack because they're afraid that their executives would drop dead if they did order one. Not that they are going to. All this is hypothetical."

Lehnhausen said, "You were a Minuteman once. You resigned when the organization was declared an illegal one. I would think. . . ."

"I'm not the Paul Eyre of that time."

"Sometimes we wonder if you're Paul Eyre at all," Lehnhausen said.

Eyre laughed. He knew what Lehnhausen was thinking. Tincrowdor had explained to him that some of the higher-ups had to be convinced that he could change into a thing that was alien to the Earth. And some of them would then conclude that the real Paul Eyre had been killed and his place taken by this thing. This thing, this creature, "this monster from outer space," had come to take over the Earth or, at least, to wreck it so that it would be helpless before the invasion that would follow.

"Science fiction stories and horror movies have conditioned people to think along these lines," Tincrowdor said. "I've thought the same thing myself, but I've observed you closely. You're the original Paul Eyre all right. At least, half the original. You may be possessed, but you're not wholly possessed."

For the first time, Paul Eyre fully realized that he was the only free man on the planet. He could do anything he wished and nobody could stop him. He could move to any country he wished, and the authorities could not stop him. Neither the U.S. nor the country in which he wished to live could do a thing. He could live where he chose, steal, rob openly, rape, and murder, and he would be unhindered.

He had no wish to do any of this, which was fortunate. But what if somebody else had had his experience? What if some immoral man had encountered that creature in the woods near that farm?

And what kind of a world would it be if everybody had his powers? Nobody would dare to threaten anybody else. But what about a quarrel in which both thought they were right? This was the usual situation. Would both arguers die? Not unless each intended physical harm to the other. Which meant that the violent one would be the one to die.

"There's nothing to talk about," Eyre said. "I'm getting tired of being bugged by you and the other government officials."

That includes the President, he thought. But he could not bring himself to say it. He still had some awe of the chief executive.

"I don't want to see you again, or hear from you any more, unless it's a national emergency. And I doubt that there's any need for that even then. The emergency will be over before you're aware of it."

"You're not God!" Lehnhausen said. "Even though there are some fanatics who claim you are!"

"I've publicly rejected those nuts," Eyre said. "It's not my fault that they pay no attention to what I say."

He looked at his wristwatch. "I have an appointment. So why don't you go now?"

"You're just a citizen . . .!" Lehnhausen said and stopped. The eyes behind the thick glasses were bulging, and his face was red.

He swallowed, took out a handkerchief, wiped his glasses and his forehead, put the glasses back on, and tried to smile. He held the handkerchief in a tight fist.

"You're safe unless you try to use violence," Eyre said softly.

"I had no such intention," Lehnhausen said. "Very well. If you won't do your duty. . . ."

"Can't, not won't."

"The result is the same. But, as I started to say, the President would like at least one assurance from you. The election will take place in a year, and. . . ."

"And you want my promise that I won't run for president," Eyre said. "But I told him that I had no such ambitions."

"People have been known to change their minds."

"I'm neither qualified nor interested. I'd make a mess of things. There was a time when I was ignorant enough to believe that I could do better than anybody else in the White House. But my horizons have broadened since then. I'm still ignorant, but not that ignorant."

"We know that you've been approached by the Democrats, the Socialist Labor Party, the Communists, and the Messianists. If you. . . ."

"If I did run, it'd be as a Republican," Eyre said. "And the first thing I'd do would be to get rid of those people who are trying to kill me. You'd be among them."

Lehnhausen turned pale, and he said, "I deny that!"

"I suspect that the man who tried to kill me this morning was one of your agents. That anti-Christ business was just to make people think he was a religious fanatic."

"You're getting paranoid," Lehnhausen said.

"A paranoiac is one who has no rational basis for suspecting persecution. I know that you've been trying to assassinate me."

"Assassination implies a political motive," Lehnhausen said. "The correct word is murder."

"You have a political motive," Eyre said. "But it's not the main motive. Good-bye, Mr. Lehnhausen."

Lehnhausen hesitated and then, slowly, pulled a paper from his coat pocket. "Would you sign a statement that you will not be a candidate?"

"No," Eyre said. "My word is good enough. Good-bye."

CHAPTER FIVE

"That's the first time you ever asked me about my middle name," Tincrowdor said. "Hadn't curiosity ever entered that dull mind of yours before?"

"I always thought it was an Indian name and that you had Indian blood and didn't want to admit it," Eyre said.

"I do have Miami Indian ancestors," Tincrowdor said. "But I'm not the least bit ashamed of it. Queequeg, however, is supposed to be a Polynesian name, though it certainly doesn't have a melodious vowel-filled substance which distinguishes all Polynesian words. I think Melville made it up. In any event, my father read a lot, even if he was an electrical engineer. His favorite book was *Moby Dick*, and his favorite character was the giant harpooner, Queequeg. So he named me after the son of the king of the island of Kokovoko. *It is not down in any map; true places never are.* So says Ishmael.

"If I'd been given any choice in the business, I would have taken Tashtego as my name. That Indian stuck to his job to the last, nailing up the defiant flag of Ahab even as the Pequod sank, and catching the wing of the sky hawk between the spar and his hammer, taking a living bit of heaven with him down to hell. A fine bit of symbolish, though rather too obvious for anybody but Melville to get away with it.

"On the other hand, my father probably knew what he was doing when he labeled my character before it was formed. Queequeg thought much about his death, and so do I. Queequeg prepared his coffin while he was still living, and so do I. His was stiff wood and carved with many strange symbols. Mine is fluid alcohol, and the carving is done with the bending of the elbow. Both of us float alive in our coffins."

Tincrowdor poured himself another drink, sniffed at it, and said, "Zounds! This is the best the world, and Kentucky, offers."

"Let's get back to the subject," Eyre said.

"The only true subject is oneself, and I never get off it. So where were we?"

"Extrapolating. And I wish you'd quit drinking. You said your memory and your creativity have been much better since you started seeing me. Your drinking had caused brain damage, and I had reversed the irreversible. Yet you continue to destroy your brain."

"Why not, as long as I can still be healed by coming into your holy presence? When you go forever, I'll quit. Or try to."

"And you think I'll go?"

"I would advise you to leave now. I don't mean tomorrow morning. I mean right now. You're staying for only two reasons, neither of which should be considered. One, you can't shuck off guilt because you'll be deserting your family, which you have done, anyway, and the sick people of this earth. Forget them. They're going to die anyway, and you can never cure all of them or anything but a small portion. Earth breeds sick humans faster than a dozen Paul Eyres could heal them. Second, you could stay here a thousand years and no mate would come. So get out to the stars and look for one."

Tincrowdor swallowed three ounces, smacked his lips, and said, "I forgot. There are two other reasons. Third, let humanity go its own way. Let it choose its own destiny, miserable as that probably will be. Man was not meant to be a flying saucer. Fourth, if you hang around this planet, you will inevitably be killed."

Eyre started a little and said, "How could they do that?"

"I don't know, but they'll figure out a way. Man's stupidity is only exceeded by his ingenuity. You're a challenge to our survival, and think tanks all over the world are working three shifts a day contriving means for your destruction. Somebody is going to come up with the solution, and you'll be dissolved."

"I don't see how."

"You've been given godlike powers, but your imagination hasn't been improved much. *Of course*, you can't see."

"Can you?"

"Don't look at me so narrow-eyed. I'm no danger to you. Not now. I quit thinking up ways. At least, I'm not telling anybody about them."

"All right," Eyre said. "I am sick of this never-ending task. It's no joy to go to bed knowing that thousands more are waiting in motel rooms to see me in the morning, that thousands more are traveling to see me the morning after. Yet, I feel that the poor devils need me, and my conscience would hurt me if I abandoned them.

"But I also feel that I am neglecting my main duty. I should be out there, looking for someone with whom I can be a true mate. Someone, or something, with whom I can share an ecstasy that you . . . human beings, I mean . . . can never know."

"One is a duty; the other is a joy. That's what you mean," Tincrowdor said.

"And my manifest duty," Eyre said.

"You talk as if you're a nation, not a person," Tincrowdor said.

"I could bear nations within me."

"Yes, you *could*," Tincrowdor said, looking as if surprise had sobered him. "You could carry millions of saucer-gametes within you. Fly over a populated city, release the yellow cloud, and hundreds, maybe thousands, would become impregnated or spermified, or however you want to put it. And that would mean the end of the human race. As we know it, anyway."

"That is what I don't understand," Eyre said. "For the sake of efficency, the gametes should be distributed among a dense population. Why was the yellow cloud released when I was the only one who could be affected?"

"We have to assume, for logical reasons, that it was an accident. You fired at what you thought was a quail, but it was the, uh, saucerperson. Your shotgun pellets wounded her and brought forth the gametes before their time."

"Yes, but why didn't I drop dead before I fired? And what about her wounds? When I saw her later, in her other form, she didn't have a scar."

"The latter first. She, and I suppose you,

have wonderful self-healing properties. If you can heal others, why not yourself? As for her vulnerability, perhaps the saucer form doesn't have the killing powers that the human form has. The gamete that fused with you has the power to protect itself while it's in a fragile form, that is, yours. The adult form, or at least the saucer form, doesn't have this. Why, I don't know, since you have it when you revert to the human form."

Tincrowdor took another drink and then said, "But perhaps you're not an adult yet. Or perhaps the adult just doesn't have the ability to kill by thought, or however it's done. Remember, when she fled the prison yard with machine gun bullets flying around her, the guards shooting at her didn't drop dead. I find that significant."

Eyre tried to keep the alarm out of his voice.

"Then why haven't they tried to kill me when I'm in that . . . saucer . . . form? They must be watching my window. They've seen me shoot in and out of it and they've tracked me with radar. I know that, because I've fed on the radar waves."

"What happened? Their instruments were missing every other wave? They didn't get a complete echo?"

"I don't know. But they must have thought something was wrong with their equipment."

Tincrowdor laughed. He said, "They didn't shoot at you because it never occurred to them that you might be lacking your powers when in that metamorph."

"Then nobody knows?"

Tincrowdor hesitated and said, "I know. At least, I suspect."

"And you've told nobody?"

"Nobody."

Eyre was not worried that their conversation was being monitored. He didn't care that the phones were tapped, but he could not endure being overheard when he was talking to the women who visited him. Two men came in twice a day and swept the apartment for electronic bugs, and he himself checked it out in the evening with equipment supplied by the FBI.

"Cross your heart and hope to die?" Eyre said, grinning.

"I'm afraid that I *would* die," Tincrowdor said.

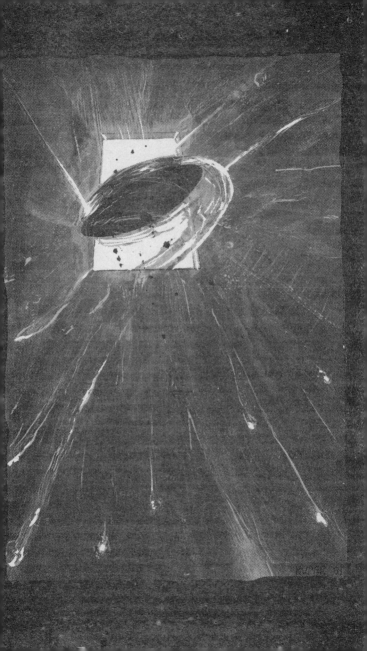

CHAPTER SIX

While racing as a tiny satellite of the earth and while sitting or walking in his apartment, Eyre had tried to communicate with the entity in his brain. Silence was the only response. Silence and emptiness. He did not feel that he was occupied. He was alone. Singular.

Yet he knew about the tests which the now dead Dr. Croker had made. The first of these had revealed that his blood and other tissues were swarming with microscopic creatures. They looked more like yellow bricks with rounded edges than anything. Then these were gone, presumably excreted, except for one, which had been located in his brain.

It was this organism which had given him
his powers to kill, to cure, and to metamorphose. This, according to Tincrowdor,
was a sort of gamete, analogous to a human
ovum. Eyre, though composed of trillions
of cells, was another gamete, the sperm.
The saucer-gamete had fused with him to
make a new individual. The fusing was not,
however, necessarily physical. It could be
solely physical. Or it could be psychosomatic.

Whatever its final stage in him, it seemed
to carry ancestral memories, and it seemed
to communicate these to Eyre through
dreams. Time and again, while sleeping, he
had visions of a glimmering green city,
many-domed, many-towered, far away
beyond fields of red flowers. Sometimes he
had seen creatures that looked like leo-
centaurs, half human, half lion. Sometimes,
he was a female leocentaur and he, or she,
mated. Sometimes, he was in saucer form
and voyaging between stars, pulling
himself along on the crumpled fabric of
space and eating light and other forms of
energy.

In the past six months, these dreams had
ceased. Did that mean that the entity was
no longer separate but had fused with him?
And if it had, why did he, Eyre, feel
unchanged, totally human? That is, he did
when he was in bipedal form. When in
saucer form, he felt almost all nonhuman,

though if someone had been able to ask him his name, he would have replied that it was Paul Eyre.

Tincrowdor had said that it was not true that Eyre was unchanged. He had a perceptiveness and a compassion he had lacked before. But that could be due to the shock of the events he had experienced. These had shaken loose qualities which had always existed in him but which, for some reason probably grounded in his childhood, he had suppressed.

"Possibly," Tincrowdor had said, "the entity is dominant when the saucer form is used. It takes over your brain then, though the possession is so subtle that you think you are in control. When in human form, you are dominant, though it is evident that the entity still uses its survival powers. However, these may be potentialities which have always existed in the human psychosoma but which only a very few have been aware of or have been able to use. Examples: so-called witch doctors or medicine men in so-called primitive societies.

"It is possible, as I've said, that these powers exist only when you're in human form. When in saucer form, you rely on speed to suvive. The only way to find out is to make a test. And you can't do that, because if you're powerless, then you'll be killed. Knowledge, in this case, would not be worth the price."

This was the dilemma which occupied much of his human time. When hurtling through air or just above it, when racing across the fields or skimming cities, he did not think of it. He felt too much joy to let terrestrial concerns into his consciousness. The joy was, it was true, tempered by a dull sadness on not finding a mate. But this intrusion took place only when dawn threatened the mid-west and he returned home.

Tonight, after Tincrowdor had left, he sped out of the window and soared vertically upward. For the first time, he determined to leave the sublunary space and to visit the moon itself. Perhaps there might be one of his kind there, though something told him that the chances were not high. It was an easy and swift journey; he was not handicapped by complex problems of orbital computation and power expenditure. All he had to do was point himself at the moon, overtake it, match his velocity with its, increase or decrease his velocity, and circle around and around it, swoop down, nestle for a while, soar up again, and streak for earth. The whole trip, according to the clock in his apartment, had taken three hours and four and a half minutes. An hour of that had been spent exploring the moon's surface.

The following Saturday and Sunday, he

visited Mars and its two moons, Deimos and Phobos.

The weekend after that, he visited Venus, but he did not stay long in its heavy, cloud-laden atmosphere. As he shot through it, battling against titanic winds and tiny particles whose nature he did not know, he detected something living far, far down. It was shadowy, huge, vaguely spindle-shaped, and it radiated danger. He curved upward in a burst of speed which brought him near the burning point. His panic did not subside until he had put himself far above the atmosphere. When he had regained his apartment and his human form, he wept and sobbed. Whatever his own powers were, he would have been caught like a mouse by a cat and destroyed in some horrible manner if he had not reacted so swiftly. That thing would have ingested him but would not have killed all of him. A piece of him would have suffered hell for eons before his last spark had fallen into darkness.

He rarely needed sleep, but this morning he was squeezed with fatigue. He lay down on the bed without putting on his pajamas and slept, though not well. Twice he woke up moaning with horror as something black and shapeless tried to pull him into itself.

The horror weighed him during the days and nights that followed. For the first time, he did not feel safe when in saucer form. If such a thing could exist on Venus, what might he find on Jupiter or Pluto?

One Saturday morning he made up his mind. He would leave Earth and the human race and go seek another of his kind. He needed the companionship they could provide, though he had no idea of what its nature would be. Whatever it was, it surely must be superior to that which men and women had given him. Or, to be fair, that which he had given them. Something in him had made him a loner, no matter how gregarious he might seem to others. He had had no true friends, people with whom he felt comfortable and intimate. His efforts at conversation had been ludicrous and boring. He felt at ease only around machines, which explained why they had taken so much of his time or why he had given them so much time. He could handle them, could analyze their malfunctions and repair them. But his acquaintances, his fellow workers, his family were enigmas. He was out of phase with them, and the one with whom he had been most intimate was a stranger whom he hated and who hated him. If he had had his present perceptiveness when he had married Mavice, he could have saved the marriage and even been happy with it. But it was too late for that now.

Maybe his meeting the saucer-sphinx thing in the woods had not been an accident. Maybe it, she, rather, had sensed that he could make ·the transition to nonhuman form easier than most humans she had surveyed. His roots were shallow and in loose soil; being torn from humanity would not be difficult or too painful for him.

There were too many maybes. He wanted certainty and knowledge, and the only way for him to gain these was to venture out after those who could give him facts.

And so, having decided, he picked up the Sunday morning paper and saw that which changed his mind again.

CHAPTER SEVEN

He read the story on page two of the A section and then phoned downstairs for Chicago and St. Louis papers. These had the same story but in more detail than the local journal.

FLYING SAUCER SEEN IN LOS ALAMOS AREA
UFO LANDS IN NEW MEXICO
RADAR AND EYEWITNESSES SEE VISITORS FROM SPACE?

"Yesterday, April 1 (April Fool's Day), at 5:32 P.M., MST, a busload of government workers saw. . . ."

". . . radar detected and held on its screen for two minutes a UFO. . . ."

". . . the pilot reports seeing the object land on top of a hill. . . ."

". . . officials refuse to make any comment. . . ."

Eyre read everything about the "conventionally shaped UFO" and then turned on the TV. Not until the five o'clock news was there any mention of the UFO, and that was a brief comment by a broadcaster who obviously thought it was a hoax. But there was a photograph of a blurred object supposedly taken by a guard near the test area. This had been the scene of a number of hydrogen bomb experiments in the late 1960's.

Eyre thought several times about leaving at once, even though it was daylight. What difference did it make now if he broke his vow to himself not to change shape until the sun had long been down? He probably wouldn't be coming back, and so what did he care that passersby might see him? Let them talk. The story would increase the amount of attention on him, anyway.

But he did not follow his impulse. He might not find her (why did he think of it as her when it might be another male?). If she were gone, had come to Earth for only a little while, he would have to go after her. But he might not find her. He had no way of determining toward what sector of space she would be flying.

However, it did not seem likely that she would stay for only a little while. She might be ready to "give birth" to a cloud of gametes and so was looking for a concentration of humans. But if this were so, why had she picked out the remote and sparsely populated Los Alamos atomic testing grounds? Had she been attracted by some residue of radiation?

As soon as night came, he would go. The skies were starting to cloud and rain was predicted. It would be dark enough for him to leave then; he would go so fast that the human eye would not recognize him as anything but a streak. The human mind would classify him as an illusion, a temporary aberration of the eye. What did it matter what they thought?

A few minutes before the sun touched the horizon, he phoned Tincrowdor. "Hello, Leo. Paul. I'm going."

There was a pause, and then Tincrowdor, in a strange voice, said, "I thought you would. But listen, Paul, I. . . ."

"Never mind. Good-bye."

"But Paul. . . !"

Eyre hung up the phone and undressed. The phone began ringing. Tincrowdor was probably calling back, but he would have nothing to say that needed hearing. He would say that Eyre's first duty was to humanity (despite the many times he'd argued against that). He would remind Eyre that it was his presence that ensured against atomic war or even a large-scale conventional war. He would . . . what did it matter what he would say?

And so he slipped into his other form like a hand into a glove and flung the gauntlet of himself against the night.

CHAPTER EIGHT

Around and around over what he thought
was northern New Mexico, he sped. The
earth was a shifting pattern of triangles and
cubes, glowing brightly, varicolored, the
hills blocks of silver nudging the chestnut
triangles around them. And then far away,
tiny, a light like that from a firefly's tail
glowed. On, off. On, off. Dash, dot. Dash,
dot. The longer pulses looked to him as if
they were scarlet musical quarter notes
written against an azure page so pale that
he could see the vague geometrical forms of
the earth behind it. The shorter pulses
looked like six-branched candelabras
enveloped in silver fuzz.

They gave him no shock of recognition.

They were not what he had expected. Certainly, they were not radiations from his "mother," the creature that had passed him in space as she traveled toward some planet circling some far-off star. But then he had seen her moving, and the shape of his kind (his kind!) changed with velocity. No, it did not actually change, but his perception of her had changed as she changed vectors. This one must be resting on the ground.

She was, he thought excitedly, waiting for him.

But why here? Why hadn't she sought him out in his apartment?

Eyre could "see" in all directions and so perceived his downward angle of flight as double amphorae burning blue. Among them were little novae of green sputtering off into violet; these indicated that he was not flying in a calm mood; he was thrilled with delight.

The pulses came faster, merged into expanding and disappearing obovoids and then became a many-rayed star with a yellow center. If he were in human form, he knew, he would see simply a saucer shape, light-gray, two feet in diameter, four inches high at the thickest part, the center. It would be lying in the middle of a plain over three miles wide; the wavering bands of purple would be cacti.

Or would it? A many-rayed star with a yellow center. There was something about that form and color that was familiar or at least should be familiar.

Where?

Suddenly, he knew.

He pulled up and away, but it was too late.

There was only one light, now, the blinding raving light of a sun. Or of atomic energy loosed, matter turning into energy, expanding.

Even as he raced away, its tongue lapping at him, he thought, How did they do it?

CHAPTER TEN

The man said, "The President did not want to commend you by letter or phone. Why I don't know, so don't ask me. I was just told to deliver the message verbally."

Tincrowdor stood looking out of a window of the living room. The man sat on a sofa with a cup of coffee in one hand. Morna, Tincrowdor's wife, was not home. The man had made certain of that before he came to the house.

Out there in the moonless night was a field, and in the field was a towering and very old sycamore tree. Near its roots was a smooth place over which new grass was growing. Below the grass lay a hard shell ripped open at one end and within were

decaying meat and worms. Only Tincrowdor knew that it was there because he
had buried it, and he intended to tell no one
about it. He did not want to repeat Eyre's
history.

Was his blood swarming with millions of
tiny yellow brick-shaped things? Probably.
He had no intention of getting a doctor to
examine his blood. This time, events would
take a different course.

He turned and said, "So you don't know
what the message means?"

The man looked alarmed. "If you try to
tell me, I'll get up and walk out."

"No sweat," Tincrowdor said. "Well, you
tell the President that mum is the word and
that he doesn't have to worry about me. Not
that he doesn't know that already. And tell
him that I'm not sorry that he can't give me
a medal. I wouldn't accept it. But you can
tell him that if I'd known he was going to
use my plan, I . . . well, anyway, tell him for
me that he's a big liar. He promised. . . ."

The man looked bewildered. Tincrowdor
said, "Never mind. Just tell him I said
thanks for nothing."

The man put the cup down and rose. "Is
that all?"

"That's all I have to say or ever will say
on the subject. Which I'll bet you're dying
to know. Which would be what *would*
happen if you did know."

The man's eyebrows rose. He picked up

his hat and said, "Good-bye, Mr. Tin-crowdor." He did not offer to shake hands. But he hesitated at the doorway.

"Did you know Paul Eyre very well?"

"As well as anyone could." .

"I'm asking because he cured my wife's terminal cancer, you know."

"I didn't know, but I can see why you can't restrain your curiosity."

"That *was* strange!" the man burst out. "Disappearing like that and no trace what-soever! And guarded by two dozen men! FBI, too! Do you think that he just took off? Or did some foreign agents . . .?"

"I wouldn't care to speculate."

"Well, at least the world will never be the same again."

Tincrowdor smiled and said, "You never spoke a truer word."

"A man like him never truly dies. He lives on in us."

"In some of us, anyway," Tincrowdor said. "Good-bye, Mr. Sands."

After the man had left, Tincrowdor poured himself another bourbon. Well, he thought, Eyre certainly knew whom he should revenge himself on. Came straight here. He couldn't have known, but he must have guessed that I originated the trap. But the president told me that the plan was rejected. And, later, I was glad that he had turned it down. I didn't really want to be responsible for Eyre's death.

When in the saucer form, the power to kill or cure by thought, or whatever, doesn't operate. So, catch Eyre in that form. And the bait? What he desired most, a mate. That rhymes, doesn't it?

Eyre told me how he perceived things, and so I knew he'd never be fooled by just a simulacrum. It would have to contain something living. And the shell did. It held a swarm of bees.

Eyre had been fooled long enough to get caught. The atomic bomb buried under the earth beneath the dummy had been triggered by a device connected to the radar. The image registered by the radar was the only one that would set the bomb off.

There were outcries from governments about illegal experimentation with bombs, even though the U.S. government had said that it was an accident. This was for public consumption. After the governmental heads had been informed, secretly, that Paul Eyre was dead, the objections were dropped, the excuses accepted.

Radar had tracked Eyre into the area of Busiris, Illinois, and he could imagine the consternation that must have caused. But when no remains were found, it had been concluded, or at least he supposed it had been, that Eyre had fallen into the river or somewhere in the woods around Busiris. A quiet search had been conducted without success. Months passed, and with these the jitters of the officials had evaporated.

There had been one thing which Tincrowdor had not understood. Eyre had had no mate, so how could he release a cloud of gametes? If the saucerperson released these, and there had been no cross-fertilization, then the gametes would contain only the genes of the mother.

After some wrestling with his mind, he had concluded that that did not matter. The being with whom a gamete fused would eventually find a mate. Or, if it did not, then it would pass on its gametes to another, who would in turn find a mate.

Or perhaps there was no mating, no cross-fertilization, not as terrestrial science defined it. Every adult form generated gametes in its body, and the purpose of these was to locate and fuse with a being of an entirely different genus. Maybe with a being of an entirely different kingdom, since the saucers might, for all he knew, be vegetables. Or some type of creature neither animal nor vegetable.

Whatever the theory, the reality proceeded unhindered.

He went to the window and lifted his glass in toast to the inert and invisible mass under the trees.

"You win, Paul Eyre. You and your kind. Soon to be my kind."

The door opened, and his wife, Morna,

entered.

He said hello and kissed her, thinking as he did so of that night when he had rubbed the yellow mercury stuff on her hand while she slept.

He did not know whether he had done it from love or hate. But he did know that he did not want to go into the unknown alone.

KUPER '81

By Philip Jose Farmer and
Leo Queequeg Tincrowdor

SPECIAL BONUS: A
COLLABORATION BY THE
AUTHOR AND A CHARACTER
FROM *STATIONS OF
THE NIGHTMARE*

OSIRIS ON
CRUTCHES

I

Set, a god of the ancient land of Egypt, was the first critic. Once he had been a creator, but the people ceased to believe in his creativity. He then suffered a divinity block, which is similar to a writer's block.

This is a sad fate for a deity. Odin and Thor, once cosmic creators, became devils—that is, critics—in the new religion which killed off their old religion. Satan, or Lucifer, was an archangel in the Book of Job, but he became the chief of demons, the head-honcho critic, in the New Testament. The Great Goddess of the very ancient Mediterranean regions, named Cybele, Anana, Demeter, depending on where she lived, became a demon; Lilith, for instance, or, in one case, the Mother of God (and who criticizes more than a mother?). But she had to do that via the back door, and most people that pray to her don't know that she was not always called Mary. Of course, there are scholars who deny this, just as there are scholars who deny the existence of the Creator.

Those were the days. Gods walked the earth then. They weren't invisible or absent as they are nowadays. A man or a woman could speak directly to them. They might get only a divine fart in their faces, but if the god felt like talking, the human had a once-in-a-lifetime experience.

Nowadays, you can only get in contact with a god by prayer. This is like sending a telegram which the messenger boy may or may not deliver. And there is seldom a reply by wire, letter, or phone.

In the dawn of mankind, the big gods in Egypt were Osiris, Isis, Nephthys, and Set. They were brothers and sisters, and Osiris was married to Isis and Set was married to Nephthys. Everybody then thought that incest was natural, especially if it took place among the gods.

In any event, no human was dumb enough to protest against the incest. If the gods missed you with their lightning or plagues, the priests got you with their sacrificial knives.

People had no trouble at all seeing the

gods, though they might have to be quick about it. The peasants standing in mud mixed with ox manure and the pharaohs standing on their palace porches could see the four great gods, along with Osiris' vizier, Thoth, and Anubis, as they whizzed by. These traveled like the wind or the Roadrunner zooming through the Coyote's traps. Their figures were blurred with speed, dust was their trail, the screaming of split air their only sound.

From dawn to dusk they raced along, blessing the land and all on and in it.

However, the gods noticed a peculiar thing when they roared by a field just north of Abydos. A man always sat in the field, and his back was always turned to them. Sometimes they would speed around to look at his face. But when they did, they still found themselves looking at his back. And if one god went north and one south and one east and one west, four boxing the man in, all four could still see only his back.

"There is One greater than even us," they told each other. "Do you suppose that She, or He, as the case might be, put him there? Or perhaps that is even Him or Her?"

"You mean 'He or She'" Set said. Even then he was potentially a critic.

After a while they quit staying up nights wondering who the man was and why they couldn't see his face and who put him there. But he was never entirely out of their minds at any time.

There is nothing that bugs an omniscient like not knowing something.

II

Set stopped creating and became a nasty, nay-saying critic because the people stopped believing in him. Gods have vast powers and often use them with no consideration for the feelings or wishes of humans. But every god has a weakness against which he or she or it is helpless. If the humans decide he is an evil god, or a weak god, or a dying god, then he becomes evil or weak or dead. Too bad, Odin! Rotten luck, Zeus! Tough shit, Quetzalcoatl! Trail's end, Gitche Manitou!

But Set was a fighter. He was also treacherous, though he can't be blamed for that since the humans had decided that he was no good. He planned some unexpected events for Osiris at the big festival in Memphis honoring Osiris' return from a triumphant world tour, SRO. He planned to shortsheet his elder brother, Osiris, in a big way. From our viewpoint, our six-thousand-year perspective, Set may have had good reason. His sister-wife, Nephthys, was unable to conceive by him and, worse, she lusted after Osiris. Osiris resisted her, though not without getting red in the face and elsewhere.

This was not easy, since Osiris' flesh was green. Which has led some moderns to speculate that he may have come in a flying saucer from Mars. But his flesh was green because that's the color of living plants, and he was the god of agriculture. Among other things.

Nephthys overcame his moral scruples by getting him drunk. (This was the same method used by Lot's daughters many thousands of years later.) The result of this illicit rolling in the reeds was Anubis. Anubis, like a modern immortal, was a "funny-looking kid," and for much the same reason. He had the head of a jackal. This was because jackals ate the dead, and Anubis was the conductor, the ticket-puncher, for the souls who rode into the afterlife.

Bighearted Isis found the baby Anubis in the bulrushes, and she raised him as her own, though she knew very well who the parents were.

Osiris strode into Memphis. He was happy because he had just finished touring the world and teaching non-Egyptians all about peace and nonviolence. The world has never been in such good shape as then and, alas, never will be again. Set smiled widely and spread his arms to embrace Osiris. Osiris should have been wary. Set, as a babe, had torn himself prematurely and violently from his mother's womb, tearing her also. He was rough and wild, white-skinned and red-haired. He was a wild ass of a man.

Isis sat on her throne. She was radiant with happiness. Osiris had been gone for a long time, and she missed him. During his absence, Set had been sidling up to her and asking her if she wanted to get revenge on her husband for his adulterous fling with Nephthys. Isis had told him to beat it. But, truth to tell, she was wondering how long she could have held out. Gods and goddesses are hornier than mere humans, and you know how horny they are.

Isis, however, had to wait. Set gave a banquet that would have turned Cecil B. De Mille green with envy. When everyone ached from stuffing himself, and belches were exploding like rockets over Fort Henry, Set clapped his hands. Four large, but minor, gods staggered in. Among them they bore a marvelously worked coffer.

They set it down, and Osiris said, "What is that exquisite *objet d'art*, brother?"

"It's a gift for whomever can fit himself into it exactly," Set said. Anybody else would have said "whoever," but Set was far more concerned with form than content.

To start things off, Set tried to get into the coffer. He was too tall, as he knew he'd be. His seventy-two accomplices in the conspiracy—Set was wicked but he was no piker—were too short. Isis didn't even try. Then Osiris, swaying a little from the gallons of wine he'd drunk, said, "If the coffer fits, wear it." Everybody laughed, and he climbed into the coffer and stretched out. The top of his head just touched the head of the coffer, and the soles of his feet just touched its foot.

Osiris smiled, though not for long. The conspirators slammed the lid down on his face and nailed it down. Set laughed; Isis screamed. The people ran away in panic. Paying no attention to the drumming on the lid from within the coffer, the accomplices rushed the coffer down to the Nile. There they threw it in, and the current carried it seaward.

III

Some gods need air. Others are anaerobic. In those days, they all needed it, though they could live much longer without air than a human could. But it was a long journey down the Nile and across the sea to Byblos, Phoenicia. By the time it grounded on the beach there, Osiris was dead.

Set held Isis prisoner for some time. But Nephthys, who loathed Set now, joined Anubis and Thoth in freeing her. Isis journeyed to Byblos and brought the body back, probably by oxcart, since camels were not yet used. She hid the body in the swamps of a place called Buto. As evil luck would have it, Set was traveling through the swamp, and he fell over the coffer.

His face, when he saw his detested
brother's corpse, went through the changes
of wood on fire. It became black like wood
before the match is applied, then red
flames, then pale like ashes. He tore the
corpse in fourteen parts, and he scattered
the pieces over the land. He was the
destroyer, the spreader of perversity, the
venomous nay-sayer.

Isis roamed Egypt looking for Osiris'
parts. Tradition has it that she found
everything but the phallus. This was
supposed to have been eaten by a Nile crab,
which is why Nile crabs are forever cursed.
But this, like all myths, legends, and
traditions, is based on oral material that is
inevitably distorted through the ages.

The truth is the crab *had* eaten the
genitals. But Isis forced it to disgorge. One
testicle was gone, alas. But we know that
the myth did not state the truth or at least
not all of it. The myth also states that Isis
became pregnant with a part of Osiris'
body. It doesn't say what part, being vague
for some reason. This reason is not
delicacy. Ancient myths, in their
unbowdlerized forms, were never delicate.

Isis used the phallus to conceive.
Presently Horus was born. When he grew
up he helped his mother in the search. This
took a long time. But they found the head in
a mud flat abounding in frogs, the heart on
top of a tree, and the intestines being used

as an ox whip by a peasant. It was a real mess.

Moreover, Osiris' brain was studded with frog eggs. Every once in a while a frog was hatched. This caused Osiris to have some peculiar thoughts, which led to peculiar behavior. However, if you are a god, or an Englishman, you can get away with eccentricity.

One of the thoughts kicked off by the hatching of a frog egg was the idea of the pyramid. Osiris told a pharaoh about it. The pharaoh asked him what it was good for. Osiris, always the poet, replied that it was a suppository for eternity.

This was true. But he forgot in his poet's enthusiasm his cold scientist's cold regard for cold facts. Eternity has body heat. Everything is slowly oxidizing. The earth and all on it are wrapped in flames if one only has eyes to see them. And so the pyramids, solid though they are, are burning away, falling to pieces. So much for the substantiality of stone.

Meanwhile, Isis and Horus found all of Osiris' body except for a leg and the nose. These seemed lost forever. So she did the best she could. She attached Osiris' phallus to his nose hole.

"After all," she said to Horus and Thoth, "he can wear a kilt to cover his lack of genitals. But he looks like hell without a nose of any kind."

Thoth, the god of writing, and hence also of the short memory, wasn't so sure. He had the head of an ibis, which was a bird with a very long beak. When Osiris was sexually aroused, he looked too much like Thoth. On the other hand, when Osiris wasn't aroused, he looked like an elephant. Usually, he was aroused. This was because the other gods left him in their dust while he hobbled along on his crutch. But Isis wasn't watching him, and so he dallied with the maidens, and some of the matrons, of the villages and cities along the Nile.

Humans being what they are, the priests soon had him on a schedule which combined the two great loves of mankind: money and sex. He would arrive at 11:45 A.M. at, say, Giza. At 12:00, after the tickets had been collected, he would become the central participant in a fertility rite. At 1:00 the high priest would blow the whistle. Osiris would pick up his crutch and hobble on to the next stop, which was, literally, a whistle stop. The maidens would pick themselves up off the ground and hobble home. Everybody else went back to work.

Osiris met a lot of girls this way, but he had trouble remembering their faces. Just as well. Humans age so fast. He never noticed that the crop of maidens of ten years ago had become careworn, workworn hags. Life was hard then. It was labor before dawn to past dusk, malaria, bilharzia, piles, too much starch and not enough meat and fruit, and, for the women, one pregnancy after another, teeth falling out, belly and breasts sagging, and varicose veins wrapping the legs and the buttocks like sucker vines.

Humans attributed all their ills, of course, to Set. He, they said, was a mean son of a bitch, and when he whirled by, accompanied by tornados, sandstorms, hyenas, and wild asses bearing leaky baskets of bullcrap, life got worse.

They prayed to Osiris and Isis and Horus to get rid of the primal critic, the basic despoiler. And it happened that Horus did kill him off.

Here's the funny thing about this. Though Set was dead, life for the humans did not get one whit better.

IV

After a few thousand years people caught on to this. They started to quit believing in the ancient Egyptian gods, and so these dwindled away. But the dwindling took time.

Female deities, for some reason, last longer than the males. Isis was worshiped into the sixth century A.D., and when her last temple was closed down, she managed to slip into the Christian church under a pseudonym. Perhaps this is because men and women are very close to their mothers, and Isis was a really big mother.

Osiris, during his wanderings up and down along the Nile, noticed that humans had one method of defeating time. That was art. A man could fix a moment in time forever with a carving or a sculpture or a painting or a poem or a song. The individual passed, nations passed, races passed, but art survived. At least for a while. Nothing is eternal except eternity itself, and even the gods suddenly find that oxidation has burned them down to a crisp.

This is partly because religion is also an art form. And religion, like other art forms, changes with the times.

Osiris knew this, though he hated to admit it to himself. One day, early in the first century A.D., he saw once more the man whose back was always turned to him. This man had been sitting there for about six thousand years or perhaps for much longer. Maybe he was left over from the Old Stone Age.

Osiris decided he'd try once more. He hobbled around on his crutch, circling on the man's left. And then he got a strange burning feeling. The man's face was coming into view.

Straight ahead of the man was what the man's body had concealed. An oblong of blackness the size of a door in a small house lay flat on the earth's surface.

"This is the beginning of the end," Osiris whispered to himself. "I don't know why it is, but I can feel it."

"Greetings, first of the crippled gods, predecessor of Hephaestos and Wieland," the man said. "*Ave,* first of the gods to be torn apart and then put together again, predecessor of Frey and Lemminkainen. Hail, first of the good gods to die, basic model for those to come, for Baldur and Jesus."

"You don't look like you belong here," Osiris said. "You look like you come from a different time."

"I'm from the twentieth century, which may be the next-to-last century for man or perhaps the last," the man said. "I know what you're thinking, that religion is a form of art. Well, life itself is an art, though most people are imitative artists when it comes to living, painters of the same old paintings over and over again. There are very few originators. Life is a mass art, or usually the art of the masses. And the art of the masses is, unfortunately, bad art. Though often entertaining," he added hastily, as if he feared that Osiris would think he was a snob.

"Who are you?" Osiris said.

"I am Leo Queequeg Tincrowdor," the man said. "Tincrowdor, like Rembrandt, puts himself in his paintings. Any artist worth his salt does. But since I am not worthy to hand Rembrandt a roll of toilet paper, I always paint my back to the viewer. When I become as good as the old Dutchman, I'll show my face in the mob scenes."

"Are you telling me that you have created me? And all this, too?" Osiris said. He waved a green hand at the blue river and the pale green and brown fields and the brown and red sands and rocks beyond the fields.

"Every human being knows he created the world when he somehow created himself into being," Tincrowdor said. "But only the artist re-creates the world. Which is why you have had to go through so many millenia with a phallus for a nose and a crutch for a leg."

"I didn't mind the misplaced phallus," Osiris said. "I can't smell with it, you know, and that is a great benefit, a vast advantage. The world really *stinks*, Tincrowdor. But with this organ up here, I could no longer smell it. So thanks a lot."

"You're welcome," the man said. "However, you've been around long enough. People have caught on now to the fact that even gods can be crippled. And that crippled gods are symbols of humans and their plight. Humans, you know, are crippled in one way or another. All use crutches, physical or psychical."

"Tell me something new," Osiris said, sneering.

"It's an old observation that will always be new. It's always new because people just don't believe it until it's too late to throw the crutch away."

Osiris then noticed the paintings half-buried in the khaki-, or kaka-, colored dust.

He picked them up, blew off the dust, and looked at them. The deepest buried, and so obviously the earliest, looked very primitive. Not Paleolithic but Neolithic. They were stiff, geometrical, awkward, crude, and in garish unnatural colors. In them was Osiris himself and the other deities, two-dimensional, as massive and static as pyramids and hence solid, lacking interior space for interior life. The paintings also had no perspective.

"You didn't know that the world, and hence you, was two-dimensional then, did you?" Tincrowdor said. "Don't feel bad about that. Fish don't know they live in water just as humans don't know a state of grace surrounds them. The difference is, the fish are already in the water, whereas humans have to swim through nongrace to get to the grace."

Osiris looked at the next batch of paintings. Now he was three-dimensional, fluid, graceful, natural in form and color, no longer a stereotype but an individual. And the valley of the Nile had true perspective.

But in the next batch the perspective was lost and he was two-dimensional again. However, somehow, he seemed supported by and integrated with the universe, a feature lacking in the previous batch. But he had lost his individuality again. To compensate for the loss, a divine light shone through him like light through a stained-glass window.

The next set returned to perspective, to three dimensions, to warm natural colors, to individuality. But, quickly in a bewildering number and diversity, the Nile and he became an abstraction, a cube, a distorted wild beast, a nightmare, a countless number of points confined within a line, a moebius strip, a shower of fragments.

Osiris dropped them back into the dust, and he bent over to look into the oblong of blackness.

"What is that?" he said, though he knew.

"It is," Tincrowdor said, "the inevitable, though not necessarily desired, end of the evolution you saw portrayed in the paintings. It is my final painting. The achievement of pure and perfect harmony. It is nothingness."

Tincrowdor lifted a crutch from the dust which had concealed it all these thousands of years. He did not really need it, but he did not want to admit this to himself. Not yet, anyway—someday, maybe.

Using it as a pole up which to climb, he got to his feet. And, supporting himself on it, he booted the god in the rear. And Osiris fell down and through. Since nothingness is an incomplete equation, Osiris quickly became the other part of the equation—that is, nothing. He was glad. There is nothing worse than being an archetype, a symbol, and somebody else's creation. Unless it's being a cripple when you don't have to be.

Tincrowdor hobbled back to this century. Nobody noticed the crutch—except for some children and some very old people—just as nobody notices a telephone pole until he runs into it. Or a state of grace until it hits him.

As for his peculiarity of behavior and thought—call it eccentricity or originality—this was attributed by everybody to frog eggs hatching in his brain.